Issue 7

EDITED BY:
Ianna A. Small

midnight & indigo
PUBLISHING

**midnight & indigo**

VOLUME 1, ISSUE 7
978-1-7379332-2-9

*midnightandindigo.com*

———————

**MANUSCRIPTS AND SUBMISSIONS**
Whether you've already been published or are just starting out, we want to hear from you! We accept submissions of short stories and narrative essays written by Black women writers. View complete submission guidelines and submit your stories online at *midnightandindigo.com*. No paper submissions please.

Cover image: kkgas/Stocksy United

Printed and bound in the United States of America.
First Printing May 2022

*"We are the earth, the land. The tongue that speaks and trips on the names of the dead as it dares to tell these stories of a woman's line. Her people and her dirt, her trees."*

~ Honorée Fanonne Jeffers, *The Love Songs of W.E.B. Du Bois*

ISSUE 7

# Editor's Note

If the events of the past two years have taught us anything, it is the value of understanding ourselves and owning our "why." Life's journey is a collection of opportunities to, as my grandmother would say, "Choose your life every day."

What I love most about the stories we've chosen for this issue, is the opportunity to connect with different souls, experiencing their lives across the diaspora and at different stages of their journeys. We are introduced to characters in the process of discovering self and defining relationships, negotiating with the past, and celebrating the "things" no one else understands.

We are proud to present eight new short stories written by Black women storytellers.

**"Life in Pixels"** by Chinwe I. Ndubuka is the story of a couple's balancing act between the marriage they present to the world and the marriage they live after suffering a miscarriage. The truth is harder to hide when a wedding requires them to travel from the United States to Nigeria for an extended visit with relatives.

**"The Lucky Ones"** by Herina Ayot was inspired by the 1958 stabbing of MLK.

In **"Laundering"** by Abigail Jordon, Wesley works in her father's laundromat as punishment for a scheme that takes place before the story's opening. On a dreary night, a problem from the past walks back into her life.

What if the people who are supposed to care for you can't see you? Your therapist thinks you only know how to be angry. Your doctor thinks you're crazy. Your significant other thinks you're not so significant. **"tongue: tied and twisted"** by angelia carey explores a key question: is there anything you can do?

**"A Woman's Place"** by Ifediba Zube explores the impact of gender roles in a contemporary African home.

In **"The Roots That Held Us"** by Quintessa Knight, Evie returns home for her family reunion for the first time since her brother's death, and finds that everything is not as she left it.

Outwardly Sarauniya has nothing to complain about in **"Life is Like A Weave"** by Hannah Onoguwe. She has her own business and lives a life of apparent leisure. Underneath it all is a desire to be accepted, as she struggles to catch a younger man's eye and tries to fit into her daughter's life.

In **"The Secret"** by Valerie Morales, Lucy Alain Carruth does the unthinkable. She pays for a white soldier to be buried in the local Black cemetery. No one can ever find out, especially her three brothers.

If you're interested in reading additional short stories and narrative essays by Black women writers, visit us at midnightandindigo.com, check out previous issues, and follow us on social @midnightandindigo. Thank you for your support. Enjoy!

# Life in Pixels

Mary stared at the image on her phone while her husband drove them home from the engagement party where their photograph had been taken and already uploaded with twenty-seven other images. She didn't dare draw attention to it. One glance from Ike could quickly take things from bad to worse. He would misinterpret what had been posted from a United States suburb and shared with the world. Soon, her family and friends in Nigeria, where day was barely breaking, would see it too. But right now, it was dark and snowing, and keeping Ike's attention on the road was safer for both of them in more ways than one.

The photograph captured them in evening attire, her head pressed against Ike's as they chorused, "Cheese!" Mary cringed at the memory of Ike's arm draped heavily over her shoulder like a soaked towel. She regretted the moment his friend's mother cheerily planted herself in front of them with her phone, camera-ready, waving her hand like a traffic warden until Mary stood closer to her husband than she'd been in weeks. She'd endured it for the seconds it took to have their photograph taken, and then hurried to the bathroom because her insides wanted out. She'd breathed deeply and slowly counted to ten. Now, looking at the merry image on her phone made her sad. It was a lie.

"Mary."

She swiped the image away, thankful it was replaced by one of the other people clinking glasses.

Ike kept his eyes on the road. "What was your favorite part of the night?"

She couldn't do this. "It's late."

"Really? I heard you laughing in the dining room. You laugh with others, but you won't talk to me?"

"I talk to you."

"You know what I mean. Actual conversation."

"It's a waste of energy."

She'd reached this conclusion when he couldn't understand why she didn't appreciate his advances in the middle of grief.

Ike flexed his fingers around the steering wheel. Mary continued swiping through the photographs. In each shot, beautifully dressed people, whether speaking or listening, snacking or sipping, or simply posing for the camera, exuded happiness. As she had. Even the deviled eggs served on an oval platter smiled through their whipped yolk centers.

She was mindful no one took photographs in the middle of a dispute when nostrils flared and ugliness shrouded even the most beautiful face. Still, the images from the party made it hard to believe the grass was not greener on the other side.

Dr. and Dr. Keller's HGTV living room with its crystal chandelier, vintage wallpaper, and large arrangement of black and white photographs had provided the perfect backdrop for a celebration of love. Mary remembered feeling like Cinderella at the ball amid such elegance, perusing the framed photographs dating back to when the Kellers were young and carefree, displaying their affection at a local ice cream hangout. Their nephew, Ike's friend, in whose honor the party was thrown, seemed to have taken after them. She'd spotted him throughout the night—and the images posted online confirmed this—with his arm around his fiancée's waist, stealing kisses when he thought no one was looking. Mary imagined he was still walking on air though the party was over and the music had stopped.

It wasn't until Ike eased the car into their driveway that Mary put away her phone. Their home was modest, quiet and dark. Too quiet and too dark. For months, she'd looked forward to having the faint glow of a night light assure their child it was okay to sleep in his own bed. Such musing had proved futile as had painting the guest bedroom powder blue. She should have been counting down the final three months to bringing her baby home from the hospital, but her hopes had been dashed in her first trimester.

While Ike brushed his teeth and climbed into his side of the bed, facing shadows on the wall, Mary exchanged her dress for a comfy nightshirt. She removed her makeup and washed her face. Looking at her reflection in the bathroom mirror, she wondered how they were going to get through an extended visit with their relatives. They had purchased their plane tickets months ago when Ike's brother invited them to his wedding, before their joy died and their problems worsened past the point of arguing.

***

Ike endured his window seat for the first leg of the journey—a seven-hour flight to London Heathrow airport. He fidgeted but couldn't get comfortable crammed in with so many people. The food and entertainment options did little to help the passage of time. Sitting still seemed absurd. He had not taken a vacation from his job as a plant manager in over a year, but that was because he'd been saving time for paternity leave. The banked time was now being spent on a trip for someone else's happy beginning. It bothered him but not as much as not being able to tell his wife. Mary kept her headphones on for most of the flight. When she slept, she lay crumpled against the hard plastic armrest between them instead of leaning on him like she used to. Their conversation was limited to that of strangers; polite phrases like "excuse me" and "is this your seat belt?"

Ike watched Mary's fingers strum a tune on her lap. Her studded wedding band shaped her finger into a figure eight. She was on the gaining side of another cycle in her battle with her weight, but she wasn't the only one who suffered following their miscarriage. They'd spent the first few days on the floor in the nursery where they held each other and cried. They'd analyzed the past and traded pity for themselves and the one they could not bear to mention by name. Fits of slumber tormented more than relieved them. Dishes piled up. Mail went unopened until one night the lights didn't work because the utility bill had not been paid. So Ike went back to work. Mary didn't. When he suggested they try again two weeks after the doctor said they could, she called him a heartless machine operator and found solace in a bag of caramel-covered popcorn.

When they eventually found themselves on Nigerian soil, standing outside the tall iron gate to Mary's childhood home, Ike knew it was more than the journey, their overweight luggage, and the assaulting heat that taxed them. Mary pressed the doorbell and fished around in her purse, unfolding receipts. He fiddled with his laptop bag, looping the strap twice around his wrist before balancing the bag against the extended handle of their largest suitcase. They had agreed to spend the first few days with Mary's family before the wedding activities went into full swing and required them to be around Ike's relatives.

The sound of rubber slippers slapping concrete on the other side of the gate caught their attention. And then a familiar voice.

"Mary?"

Mary straightened. "Ma."

They heard Anna Okeke's joyful scream and the clink of the metal bolt she slid aside. The gate opened. They turned up the corners of their lips.

***

Mary watched her mother's face come into view, increasing like the phases of the moon. Her mother looked mostly the same as when Mary and Ike visited two years ago. Though her skin seemed a little worn, her cheeks still rounded out like fried buns when she smiled.

"Come in darlings!" Anna said, barely letting them through the gate before enveloping each one in a tight hug.

Mary smiled through tears, remembering what it felt like to be held.

"What's this?" her mother asked, fingering Mary's short twisted hair.

Mary playfully pushed her mother's hand away but didn't let go. "It's style."

Her mother raised her brows in mock enlightenment. "Wait till your father returns from the shop. Ike my son, welcome. Thank God for journey mercies."

Each took a suitcase and headed inside, where the peppery smell of stew greeted them. The living room was mostly as Mary remembered it. The bookcase contained more figurines and greeting cards than books. Pillows sewn from leftover George material used to make outfits dotted a new settee. Framed photographs hung from the walls. Mary skipped over her four-year-old wedding photograph.

At her mother's insistence, Mary sat with Ike on the settee while her mother went to get food. The royal treatment usually only lasted the first day of a visit.

"How does it feel to be home?" Ike asked.

This house didn't remind Mary of what she'd lost. If pregnant, she would have enjoyed twice the fuss from her mother. She looked at Ike and tried to muster warm feelings. Nothing. "It's nice."

Anna returned with a tray bearing two covered deep ceramic dishes, dinner plates, and cutlery. She set them on a low table in front of Ike and Mary. Lifting the glass lids dripping with condensation, Anna revealed white rice and tomato stew loaded with chicken and oxtail, Mary's favorite.

"Thank you, Ma," Mary and Ike chorused.

Mary spooned some rice onto a plate before asking Ike, "Is this okay?"

She knew he read the discomfort in her eyes. Ike had long been serving himself, microwaving portions from the meals she made during the day and stored in the fridge. Sometimes she waited until he arrived home from work and ate with him at the dining table. Other times, she ate alone in the basement in front of the television. It depended on how she felt. Before their loss, they would both come home from work and figure out dinner, eat together, and talk about their day.

"That's fine," he said. "Thank you."

"What's wrong?" Anna asked.

Ike shook his head. "Nothing, Ma. I ate too much airplane food."

The question resurfaced the next morning when Mary sat on a low wooden stool in the kitchen, her feet and calves hugging a large wooden mortar in front of her. She held the pestle, as long as her arm, out of the way while her mother added hot peppers and coarsely chopped red onions to the mortar.

"Mary, what's the matter?" Anna asked.

"How?" Mary said, thankful Ike and her father were outside walking the compound, talking politics. She pounded the vegetables, gently at first, to keep them from leaping out of the mortar or bursting stinging juices into her eyes.

"With your marriage."

Mary curled her left hand loosely around the upper part of the pestle, and, a few inches down, tightly gripped the pestle with her right hand. She swirled the pestle's base in furious circles, crushing the vegetables against the wood. It made for longer prep time, but Mary could see one reason her mother rarely used her food processor. This felt more authentic with more of herself involved. Maybe she would have gotten further with her therapist if there was a mortar and pestle in the room.

"We're okay."

Her mother sat on a stool next to her and lay half of a large African yam on a cutting board across her lap. She cut it crosswise four times with a knife. "There is a reason we say for better or for worse. Everyone experiences them. Sometimes a big smile and an elaborate gele standing high and wide on a woman's head for all to see can disguise the misery she's in. Same for men."

"Ma, we're all going to wear elaborate headscarves for the wedding," Mary said. Ike's brother had long sent them photographs of the silvery blue headscarves their female family members were to wear. Ike had followed up by sending money to his sister, who promised to have outfits sewn for them in time.

"Is it the baby?" Anna asked. She rotated the first yam section around like a Ferris wheel on her palm, peeling off the rough skin with her knife.

Mary suspected her mother avoided her gaze to encourage her to talk. For the first few phone calls with her mother after the horror, her mother did most of the talking, saying things would get better, and Mary sniffed. Soon after that, Mary focused the calls on the weather and her father's shop. "It's been hard."

Anna pursed her lips and nodded thoughtfully. "You'll be fine. Be kind to yourself. And Ike."

"I'm doing what I can, Ma." It was mostly true. Possibly not. "It's not like you—I—can just go to the store and get a replacement."

"I know."

"You don't." Mary spun the pestle over the mushy ingredients. No one understood. A part of her had died. DEAD. She just wanted to get through this trip, go home and hide out in her basement. Her biceps hurt, but she kept swirling the pestle.

"It's enough," Anna said. She lifted her cutting board and walked to the sink.

Mary watched her mother's motions as she peeled the remaining yam slices, cut them into large pieces, washed and added them to a pot of boiling smoked fish on the stove. When Anna returned to the center of the kitchen, Mary raised the pestle with both hands so she could scoop out the ingredients and add them to the pot along with other seasonings. "I'll be fine," Mary said to break the silence.

"Amen."

After some minutes, Anna used a fork to confirm the yam was cooked. She added a dollop of vibrant orange-red palm oil. Fresh nchanwu leaves from the garden went in last, giving the pepper soup its characteristic scent and flavor. "Come and taste."

Mary took the loaded spoon her mother offered. "Very good, Ma. Much better than my potato and dried herb version."

"I'll dry some nchanwu for you to take back. Improvising is better than nothing."

***

The taxi rocked Ike against Mary as it made its way in and out of what the driver apologized for as a pothole but would be better described as a crater in the road. Mary muttered something about government irresponsibility. Ike didn't mind. It was day four of their trip and they had barely touched each other. The pothole was doing him a favor.

He'd helped his in-laws fix things around the house while Mary accompanied her mother on trips to the market and hair salon. In the evenings, they'd all gathered in the living room but only truly watched television together in the moments Mary looked up from her phone. She claimed it was easier to chat with her friends and relatives now that they were in the same time zone. At night, Ike and Mary lay side by side listening to the sound of generators and traffic. The heat didn't encourage snuggling, but that hadn't swayed them before. Ike directed the taxi driver on the last few turns and hoped the wedding atmosphere at his family's property would be on his side.

The taxi parked in front of a duplex graced with black-framed balconies on the upper level and vibrant foliage on the ground. Shouting erupted from the left half where Ike's brother, Nnamdi, lived. His parents occupied the right half when they were in town and not in their house in the village. By the number of parked cars, it was evident both units were entertaining guests. Ike wanted to run out of the taxi like a soccer player rushing onto a field, but Mary sat rigid.

"Are you ready?" he asked.

"Sure."

"Bobo!" Ike's sister screamed as she bounded out of the building.

Ike grinned. His sister, Kelechi, had been teasing him with the nickname commonly used for good-looking men since he returned from his first semester in university with a girlfriend. He opened his arms wide and Mary stepped aside. Kelechi hugged Mary first. A shocked smile lit up Mary's face and warmed Ike's heart.

"Sisi!" Kelechi cried, greeting Mary with the female version of Bobo before hugging Ike. "I saw your photo on Facebook. That silver dress at the party. Stunning. My brother is taking good care of you."

"Thank you," Mary said, her expression retreating into her polite front.

Ike treasured the memory of his friend's engagement party where Mary wore the floor-length lace dress that garnered many likes, his included. She looked just as lovely now in a yellow sheath dress. "She's the one who makes me look good."

"Brother!" Nnamdi shouted from the door.

Nnamdi and his fiancée, Ronke, emerged holding hands, followed by Ike's parents and an older couple. Ronke's friend lingered in the doorway. After hugs and pleasantries, Ike's parents and their guests retired to their side of the building. Everyone else went into Nnamdi's unit.

Inside, Ike gasped at the sight of two of his and Nnamdi's college friends, reigniting the cheering. They hugged and shouted nicknames. Ike could barely believe how happy he felt just to see friends with whom he'd shared four years of hostels and classes and everything in between. They last saw themselves at his wedding. The men calmed down long enough for the two friends to greet Mary and ask how she was doing. Then the baritone voices quickly grew louder with every recollection and question. Kelechi linked her arm through Mary's and led the women upstairs. Ike hoped joy was infectious.

***

Mary and the other women settled in one of the guest bedrooms. The men's banter filtered through the shut door. It reminded Mary of the excitement that surrounded her wedding; the cooking and entertaining, the friends and family coming and going, the planning and cross-checking, and the hopes and dreams that kept her going like an energizer bunny, so much so she took a sleeping pill the night before her wedding. If someone had said she'd be where she was now—mourning a baby and ready to turn her back on her marriage—she wouldn't have believed it.

"That's a very happy bunch," Ronke said, dropping to her knees in front of two open suitcases on the floor.

Mary sat with Kelechi on the edge of the bed. Ronke's friend sat on a chair.

"Two days till 'I do,'" Kelechi said.

"I know!" Ronke laughed nervously. "I have a bunch of to-do lists to finish and these remaining dresses to get to their owners. Tomorrow, I'll get some pampering with my bridesmaids. Saturday, I'll be a bride. And a wife." She sighed.

"You're tired-happy," Mary said with a sympathetic smile. "The tired part will pass."

Their gazes settled on the suitcases. One held teal dresses and little gift boxes for the bridesmaids. The other contained traditional attire in two color combinations for the two families. Mary recognized the purple and silver material for the groom's Igbo family. It would be complemented with silvery-blue headscarves for the women and traditional red felt hats for the men. The attire in the navy blue and pink fabric would distinguish the bride's family accessorized with champagne-colored *ase oke*, characteristic of Yoruba culture. The *ase oke* had been sewn into wraps and headscarves for the women, or *agbada*—wide-sleeved overalls—and hats for the men. Ronke searched through the bridesmaid dresses until she found the one she handed her friend along with a gift box.

Kelechi retrieved a duffel bag from the wardrobe and set it at Mary's feet. "This is yours and Ike's."

Mary unzipped the bag and pulled out a traditional long shirt and a pair of trousers. She laid them aside and pulled out a dress, holding it up by the shoulders.

"Do you like it?" Kelechi asked.

It was a free flowing kaftan. Elaborate embroidery tapered from the shoulders to about where Mary's belly button would be. She loved *bubus*. She owned more than a handful of the comfortable gowns. However, this particular piece was a maternity dress. She and Kelechi had joked about how it had to fit her baby bump without making her look like a cow.

A look passed between Kelechi and Ronke.

"It's nice," Mary said. The *bubu* was well made. She was just not feeling it. It was no one's fault. She could have asked Kelechi to change the design to a fitted mermaid style as soon as she realized she wouldn't need so much fabric, but she'd been in no position to talk to in-laws. Besides, her weight had fluctuated so much, the situation could have been worse. She folded the dress neatly and laid it on her lap. "It's exactly what I asked for. Thank you."

"Are you sure? We can alter it," Ronke insisted. "I know a woman."

"In two days?"

They'd just met, and Mary didn't want to add to Ronke's to-do list.

"It will cost a bit, but she works wonders."

Mary traced a swirl of embroidery with her finger. She could have been so heavily pregnant that she might not have made the trip. But she wasn't. She was here. She put on a smile and looked up.

"It's fine, Ronke," she said. "What style wedding dress did you get?"

Ronke hesitated, then said, "It's a huge ball gown. I've always wanted one."

Mary nodded. Her smile crumpled and her eyes watered.

"Mary?"

"Don't mind me," Mary said. The waterworks usually sprung on her in private. Tears slid down both cheeks. "You'll be a beautiful bride."

"Sweetheart!" Kelechi hugged Mary's shoulders. "I'm so sorry."

Mary wanted to say, "Me too," but she couldn't form the words. This was the ugly cry people talked about. She leaned against her sister-in-law and wept and immediately found herself surrounded. Ronke tearfully knelt in front of her, clutching both her hands. Ronke's friend rubbed her back. They stayed huddled together until Mary needed a tissue so she could blow her nose and breathe.

***

At the sound of footsteps descending the stairs, Ike set down his drink and looked up. Mary clutched a duffel bag and a small plastic bag of chin-chin, cubed pastries. No Nigerian wedding was complete without chin-chin. He was about to jokingly ask how Mary got her hands on the snack when he saw her eyes. Her eyelids were puffy. The whites of her eyes—now tinted pink—glistened. And she'd reapplied lipstick, something she did to distract from tired eyes. Ike stood up, knowing she read the question on his face. She very slightly shook her head. Taking the duffel bag, he bid everyone goodnight.

In his parents' spare bedroom, Ike sat on the edge of the bed and waited.

"Ronke gave us chin-chin," Mary said, handing him the plastic bag. She pulled out clothes from the duffel bag and looked for hangers in the wardrobe. Holding up her dress, she ran her free hand down a thick fold. "They made it well, right?"

It looked good to him, but he didn't have her fashion sense. He remembered when Kelechi called and asked for their measurements. Mary told her to have the tailor use his best judgment, and Kelechi assured Mary the tailor had served pregnant—

Mary's eyes brimmed with tears. He hadn't seen her cry in weeks. It had been wrath or apathy. He saw now her pain, still very real like escaped molten lava. While music played downstairs, Mary confessed she'd cried with the women over this dress that was more than a dress. Ike listened.

***

At the wedding ceremony, Mary sat next to Kelechi with other members of the groom's family. Airy piano hymn music filled the church. Ike stood with Nnamdi, the best man, and three other groomsmen at the right side of the altar awaiting the bridesmaids and Ronke. The men looked dashing in their black suits and ties. Cream rose boutonnieres pinned against their lapels complemented the white and green flower arrangements on both sides of the altar. Mary remembered the butterflies she'd felt in her stomach as she'd stood outside a chapel door with her father at her own wedding. Now a guest, she smoothed her dress over her knees, letting the *bubu's* abundant fabric cascade on either side of her studded blue heels.

She watched Ike tug on his left shirt cuff and steal a glance at his watch. The bride was late as they'd expected. So were half the guests. Ike caught Mary's gaze and winked. She gave a slight smile. That morning as she stood in her slip staring at the dress on a hanger, he said she was the most beautiful woman in the world and apologized again for not giving her heart more time to heal.

"Ooh," a woman on Mary's right groaned.

Mary turned to see the unfamiliar relative pull her head away from the outstretched hand of an infant on her lap. The little girl, dressed in a cute floral dress and lace headband, latched one chubby hand on the woman's neckline, using it to steady herself, and reached further up.

"My sister," the woman said. "*Abeg*, hold my daughter for me, let me make myself decent before everyone arrives." She handed the child over with both hands.

Even more startling to Mary was how her own hands opened up like the petals of a morning glory at dawn. She set the girl on her lap facing her, but the child wouldn't bend her dimpled knees to sit down. Her tiny mouth turned into a downward pout. *Please, don't cry.* Mary held the infant up and patted her back. She could feel herself starting to sweat. The last time she held a child was before she was pregnant.

The little girl turned to her mother who shook out her headscarf to the tune of *Great is Thy Faithfulness.* This action revealed flattened hair wrapped into one rugged braid tucked in at the nape of the woman's neck. Mary raised an eyebrow. They were in public public, not ladies' bathroom public where this type of behavior was permissible.

"My dear, with all this social media," the woman said, "you don't know where your photograph will end up, and this girl didn't let me tie this thing well this morning."

The woman pulled a compact mirror out of her purse and laid it on her lap. She smoothed her hand over the crinkled papery fabric laying half on her lap and half on the chair next to her. She folded the scarf diagonally and flung it over her head.

"Social media indeed," Mary said. She didn't have to look to know people were watching.

The infant uttered three random syllables. She looked into Mary's face and then higher up at Mary's headscarf securely tied in place by Ike's mother that morning. The child reached past Mary's ear.

"No, no, no." Mary grabbed the little hand. The pudgy fingers that curled around hers were so soft she uncurled them and looked at the dainty creases in the infant's skin. The girl uttered more syllables and gave a two-tooth smile. "Hey, beautiful," Mary sang.

The little girl gurgled something and began bouncing on Mary's lap.

"She likes you," the girl's mother said, holding a pin between her teeth as she twisted loose ends of the headscarf, creating elephant ears on both sides of her head. "That's a good sign." The woman tucked one elephant ear under the other behind her head and inserted the pin. The music changed to *How Great Thou Art*. As the bridesmaids began their procession down the aisle, the woman fluffed and knotted and tucked the fabric into a remarkable headdress. "How is it?"

Mary reached over and tucked in a thick fold of fabric above the woman's forehead until it matched the rest of the defined folds running across her head. "Lovely."

The Wedding March started. Mary returned the baby to her mother's outstretched arms and rose to welcome Ronke. She smiled for many reasons.

***

It was hot outside. Mary stood next to Ike on the large front steps of the church, listening to someone call out the order of photographs. She'd joined Ike in the groom's family photograph and watched Ike pose in the groomsmen and groom's alma mater photographs. Now it was the bride's friends' turn. Each shot took a while longer after the professional photographer's shot because people posing swapped phones with on-lookers so they could have their own record.

"Do you know how much longer?" Mary asked, dabbing her face with a handkerchief.

"Just a few more, I think," Ike said. He called to a man walking by. "Please take a photo for me."

Ike handed over his phone and extended his hand to Mary. She took it, not wanting to keep the stranger waiting while she pondered what this meant. Her husband led her to a grassy spot in front of a flower hedge. He hugged Mary's waist, cinching her *bubu*.

"Hold me too tight and you just might feel me sweat," she said.

He playfully squeezed her side and loosened his grip. "Don't worry. There's air conditioning in the reception hall. Plus we have winter to look forward to."

Mary looked up at his grin and saw a fondness that had almost always been there. He deserved kindness. She turned to smile at the camera just as someone walked across the front of them.

"Take it before another person comes," Ike said to the man with his phone.

"Or before my heels sink all the way into the ground," Mary added.

"I did." The man returned Ike's phone.

Mary cringed. "We weren't ready."

"Those are the best."

She peered at the screen in Ike's palm and saw a softness in her captured gaze as she'd looked up at Ike. Her smile was not nearly as wide as his, but it was there, and she didn't feel betrayed by it. "Hmm."

"I know." Ike thanked the man and tucked his phone into his pocket. "Let's find air conditioning."

Mary reached for the crook of his arm. "Sounds good to me. Once I cool down, I'll tell you about the woman who sat next to me."

# The Lucky Ones

Once when I was 9, my mother threatened to beat me for growing too fast. This wasn't the first nor the last time she would make that threat, but she never followed through. Now, looking back at that time in Savannah when the whole world was crumbling under the weight of the Great Depression, Daddies were shooting themselves through the mouth, and Black folks were still less than half a man, I don't blame her for wanting to keep her baby girl young, pure, and innocent.

It was a playful threat. Harvest season finished and I came to the kitchen on the first day of school wearing my new periwinkle dress mother had sewn for me. My hair had grown a whole four inches in the Georgia heat, and I didn't think matching cornbraids suited me anymore for the first day of the fourth grade. I parted it on the side and used mother's curlers to shape bouncing curls around my face. I hadn't gotten my period yet, but I did notice my chest growing and when I walked into the kitchen, my mother stopped frying the bacon and stared at me like I was a foreign child.

"My little girl is disappearing before my eyes and I refuse to stand here and watch," she had said.

"Mommy, don't be silly. I'm in fourth grade now. I may as well look the part."

She stuck her hip out and perched her fist on it. "Well, I'll be damned. Listen here, be prepared to find another home if you grow one more inch or lose another ounce of baby fat, because if I see it, I'll beat the black off you. I'll beat you till you're dead."

"You will not, Mommy!" I giggled. "Besides, it's all that good food you feed me that has me growing nice and strong, and Daddy says I'm growing up to be beautiful just like you, so I guess it's your fault."

She returned to the bacon, paired it with cornbread, and plated my breakfast. "Yeah, well, you tell your daddy, as much time as he spends away from home, I gotta keep one person in the house loving and needing me the same way they did in the beginning." She pushed the plate across the table. "Hurry up and eat your breakfast, girl." Then she smoothed my hair behind my ear and got one more look at me. "You are beautiful, though. You certainly are."

Mommy talked like this often, but maybe I remember this day so vividly because it was the day I met Zola.

I left school that day, the sun hidden in clouds, wearing my periwinkle dress, my burlap bag draped across my shoulders. By this time, my curls had fallen, my hair just a dingy mop around my face, and I had wished I wore the cornbraids after all. Memphis Black, another nine-year-old, followed behind me with his band of friends taunting me as children sometimes do.

"What, chu think you cute in that blue dress? You ain't cute."

I kept walking, ignoring his comments.

"She think she cute, don't she Otto? Didn't you see her at school today, just raising her hand every time the teacher asked a question. Cute and smart. Problem is, it ain't gon do you no good, cus you ain't nuttin but a little girl. Little girls ain't good for shit."

I didn't budge or turn, but I did pick up my pace a little just a few steps ahead of them.

"Hey. Hey, Reenie. You hear me talking to you?" Then I felt a rock or a pebble hit me in my backside, and I flinched and turned abruptly.

"Leave me alone. I ain't messin with you. Why you gotta be messin with me?" I said.

"You answer me when I speak to you," Memphis said.

"I don't have to say anything to you."

I turned to continue walking, and then he shoved me. He shoved me from the back, pushing me to the ground and soiling my periwinkle dress. The boys laughed. Now on all fours, I held my tears back and dug my fingers into the mud, preparing to hurl a mound of dirt at Memphis. But that's when I heard the older girl. She had been on the road behind us, coming from the same school.

"Memphis, didn't your Daddy teach you to keep your hands off girls?" she shouted, rushing over. "Oh I forgot. You ain't got one." Then she drew her fist back and slugged him in the jaw so hard, it sent poor Memphis tumbling backward.

"Oh come on, Zola, why you startin stuff?" one of the other boys said.

"I ain't start nothing." She grabbed him by the collar tight and pulled him in close. "He started it, and I'm just finishing it. See, I got a Daddy.

And my daddy taught me not to be no pussy." Then she made a coughing sound and spit in his face, the saliva running from his eye down the length of his cheek. By this time, I had stood up, unsure whether to run or watch. "Y'all get outta here. That way." She pointed in the opposite direction. "We don't want you walking with us no more."

Memphis and the boys gathered themselves and stood in their tracks, Memphis holding the side of his jaw where it was nearly shattered. "Aww man Zola, we going home too," he said.

"You ain't walking this way. I guess you better find another way." Then she looked at me and motioned for me to follow her. "Come on, I'll walk you home. Looks like you might need it."

I followed the girl, quiet for the first few moments, unsure of what to say and sad that my dress was ruined.

"Why you let that boy talk to you like that?" she said finally.

"I don't mind him," I said, wiping flecks of dirt away from my face. "Sticks and stones can break my bones, but words don't hurt nothin."

"Yeah but if you don't stop him, he just gon keep on. You know the boy likes you. That's why he does what he does. He just wants attention. He don't get none at home."

"Well if he likes me, why don't he just say that?"

"Cus he's dumb. They all are. These boys ain't got no training in how to handle a woman."

"How do you know so much? How old are you and how come I ain't never see you before?"

"I'll be twelve on my next birthday. I don't always come to school. I come when I want to. Most times, I don't want to."

"Well where do you live?"

"On Scarlett Street, the dead end behind the church and down the road from the talking creek."

"The one filled with all the toads?"

"That's the one. Ain't another I know about. There's magic in the water. If you get down close and touch the edge of your ear to the stream, it talks to you."

"That's just a myth."

"Only people say that are the ones that can't hear it. Ugly people, evil people. People like Memphis Black. I know he can't hear it."

We crossed a clearing and the dying grass crumbled under our feet. "Do you hear it?" I asked her.

"All the damn time."

"What does it say?"

"Well, like today I went out there in the morning and it say I should come to school today because little ugly Memphis Black was gon be picking on some girl too cute to defend her own self. So I came. And you're lucky." She stopped and extended her hand. "I'm Zola."

That's how I met Izola Ware nearly ninety years ago on the first day of school at the end of the summer in 1928, and she's still the hero that saved me from little ugly Memphis Black even if the New York Times says different.

I woke up today, just like I do every day, put on my mustard-colored slippers, worn around the edges, and sat at the kitchen table where my granddaughter Patricia prepared my breakfast the same way mother did in Savannah so many years ago. Today, we had buttered toast and jam, scrambled eggs, and orange juice so thick with pulp I nearly choked on my first sip. The air outside the Jersey City apartment is different than it was in Georgia, still frigid in March and sharp like the blade on the 7-inch ivory-handled steel letter opener they say Zola used to stab that man back in '58.

Zola died last week in Queens. She was ninety-eight years old. I saw the paper just sitting there beside my plate of food, and just a moment after I opened it and read that headline staring back at me, I wished I hadn't. The news of Zola's death was a thick knuckled hand reaching down my throat and tightening a fist around my vocal chord and all my insides. It took my breath away.

*Izola Ware Curry, Who Stabbed King in 1958, Dies at 98*

The headline was eerily reminiscent of another newspaper headline from that fateful year when the incident occurred. Back then, I was still in Georgia, raising three babies and dancing with my man each night to Ray Charles and Little Richard singing about love, lust, and rock and roll. Zola, by that time, was just a memory, a childhood friend I had loved and then lost, not to death but to the world and its cruel hand.

I spent fourth grade letting her love me, and in the years thereafter, I was the one loving her. I stopped by her house on Scarlett street to pick her up for school each day, and we walked there and back talking about light-skinned boys, Black mamas, and cigarettes. The next year, Zola stopped going to school for good. She said her mama and daddy needed her to start working in the field all year round. She had a litter of younger brothers and sisters to help raise.

Zola had a way with her where everything she said came out of her mouth unexpectedly and all at once. One time, when we were eating peaches on the bank of the creek, just biting and chewing and tossing the pits in silence, the toads croaking, and the smooth hum of the water singing a tune, Zola told me she was pregnant as if she was commenting on the weather. If she had said it as I was swallowing, I might have choked to death, but she said it instead just after I had tossed my last pit and had reached into our pile of picked peaches between us to clean off another peach on my pants leg.

"What?" I asked her, confused.

"What chu gon deaf or something? I'm pregnant."

"How?"

"I had sex. How you think?" Zola was fourteen years old then.

"With who? When?" I said, wide-eyed and jaw-dropped.

"Anybody ever tell you you ask a ton of questions? Which answer you want first?"

I stopped eating peaches and looked at Zola for an explanation, still shocked at the news. I knew babies came from having sex but that was something I wasn't even thinking about doing. "Who jazzed you?"

She took a breath like I was wearing her out and then turned to face me and counted out on her fingers.

"William Holly. Walter Dumas. Dale."

"Dale?"

"Yes. Dale Clark. It's probably his."

"Dale Clark, the Clark's boy that stay over on Blackgum?"

"Reenie."

"Zola, that boy is twenty years old."

"And? What that got to do with anything? He's the only one stayed in me long enough for me to feel anything, so I figure the baby is probably his. Maybe not. But probably. Course it could also be my daddy's. He been jazzin me since I was nine, but I ain't never get pregnant before so maybe something's wrong with him."

"Does Dale know?"

"Not yet?"

"Zola, what chu gon do?"

"When?"

"When the baby comes?"

"I don't think that far ahead."

I envied Zola and felt sorry for her all at the same time. Nothing seemed to bother her all that much unless it was all an act. It wasn't until three years later that I realized it probably was. She lost Dale's baby before it was born. All I know is that I went to Scarlett street one afternoon after school, and her mama said she was sick and wouldn't be coming outside for a while. Almost two weeks later, I saw her wading waist-deep in the talking creek, straight-faced and washed out.

"Zola that chu? You know I been missing you. Your mama said you was sick or something? I thought maybe you had the baby."

She didn't turn to face me, just kept wading in the water, the leaves and toads making way for her.

I came closer and removed my shoes to dip my toes in. "You okay Zola?"

"You think babies go to heaven?" she asked me, still staring blankly ahead. And then I knew.

I never mentioned her baby again, but I wondered after I had children of my own if Zola ever cried for hers. There is something significant that mothers feel that they never can quite articulate. It's a constant fear that their children will die before they do. It's a fear that begins before the child emerges from the womb, at the first signs of movement within. There is life there, and there is a latent notion, an inevitable fact that all life as we know it comes to an end. So a fear is birthed then and there, when a mother-to-be awakes from slumber to feel her unborn child fluttering about, a heartbeat in sync with her own, that this life will at some point end and she is determined to do all within her power to prevent it. The fear lingers throughout the years, the child taking his first steps, uttering his first words, it wanes at some points, taking a backseat to more immediate concerns, but it is always there, a quiet guest poking its head out and raising its hand to speak at some expected and other unexpected moments. The fear is ever-present, even after the child is grown, perhaps married with children of her own. It never leaves unless and until the horrid thing actually happens, and the child dies. While I have never experienced this kind of pain, I imagine it is both a horribly miserable thing to endure, and yet also and simultaneously a relief to finally be rid of the fear that has been ever-present for so many years.

Zola, having lost her baby before it took its first breath, was the lucky one. She was spared the immense fear that could have made her condition worse than it already was. I believe Zola lived in fear for most of her life. Her years before me were always somewhat of a mystery. She never shared details of her parents, her father's incessant need to have her, her mother's silence. Zola lived in survival mode for so long that she lost the ability to see beyond the moment.

*I don't think that far ahead.* Those were not only her words in response to my inquiry about her plans at the news of her pregnancy, but also a recurring theme in her life. I suppose things returned to normal after the baby that never was. We still skinny-dipped in the talking creek, and I read to her on lazy Saturdays.

She met James Curry one day when she was seventeen, I, fourteen and a half.

We were coming from church, a place Zola only reluctantly joined me. I wore a collared white dress with lavender flowers on it. I don't exactly remember what Zola wore that day, but I'm sure it was something plain, a solid blue or brown dress, her hair combed backward with a band securing it. We walked, Zola's thin arm around my waist, mine around her shoulders.

"I saw you looking over at Gabe Smith when we were sposed to be closing our eyes talking to God," Zola said.

"I wasn't looking at Gabe Smith. That boy was looking at me."

"How would you know if you wasn't looking at him?"

I smiled sheepishly. "You know, Zola, I'm too young for all that stuff. I still got my head in my books. I got the whole rest of my life to be worried about boys."

"Yeah okay. But Gabe is cute though. He ain't my type. Young, a lil scrawny, and too shy for my liking. You be waiting all day for him to make a move. But he is cute."

We rounded the corner and passed Sam's market, the little commissary with a green awning that sold fruit, cigarettes, and soda pop. A crew of boys was out front smoking cigarettes, brown-skinned and wide-eyed. James Curry nodded his approval as we passed by, sucking on his stick and letting out a murmur like his mama had just set down a plate of pork chops in front of him.

Zola and I, still wrapped around each other didn't pay him no mind, but he left his squad and joined our stride alongside Zola.

"Look here, you two fine ladies too fine to be walking out here all by yourself."

"What's it to you?" Zola asked him.

"Gentleman like me cares about your safety."

"This is the Lord's Day. Don't nobody hurt nobody on the Lord's Day," Zola said.

"I know one thing; they be a fool to hurt you."

Zola stayed quiet, held me closer, and kept her stride from slipping.

So James continued. "What's your name, pretty girl? You too pretty not to be smiling."

Zola tried to stay mum, but then James brushed her free hand with his, then grabbed it, stopped walking, and held her back. "Stop for a minute. Ain't you got a second to acknowledge a brother acknowledging you?"

We stopped. Zola released her hold on me and turned to face him.

"What I got to say to get you to smile?" James kept on. "What, you shy? You remind me of a Georgia peach."

That didn't make a bit of sense to me, so I turned my nose up and said, "What does that mean?"

"That means your sister here is tough on the outside, but I'm sure she's tender and sweet on the inside. I just got some peeling to do."

"That ain't my sis—"

"That's all right Reenie." She stepped in closer to him, still straight-faced. Walked right up to him, her face just inches from his. "He thinks he can read me so well. Let's see how much he knows me. What you think I'm gon do now...what chu say ya name was?"

He didn't budge, just drew on his cigarette, blew the smoke up to the sky, and returned her stare.

"James."

"James," she repeated. "Jamesy, I ain't never been shy." Then she reached under his chin and pulled it in close, wrapping her lips around his for at least four seconds before releasing them. "And I ain't predictable."

James drew the back of his hand across his mouth and replaced the cigarette between his lips. He took a long drag, again blew the smoke up to the sky and then said, "Well then, you my kind of girl."

Zola just turned around, returned her arm to my waist, and resumed walking.

"How can I find you, pretty girl?" he yelled to her.

"You can't. I'll find you," Zola said without turning or breaking her stride.

"Well at least tell me your name. Hey..."

Zola stayed quiet, so I did too.

"Hey!" James was left yelling in the distance.

Later that night, I snuck away to the creek where Zola was washing her feet, sitting on the bank, naked. The sun had just set and I didn't have much time before Mommy would come looking for me.

"That was real brave of you Zola, kissing that man like that," I said, sitting next to her and drawing my feet up to my chest.

"That's just letting him know who's in control." She reached down and splashed the cool water over her toes. "When I was little I let a lot of people hurt me. Somewhere along the way, I decided not to do that anymore."

"Why are you like this?" I asked her. "You don't always have to be so tough. Everyone doesn't want to hurt you. Some people might want to love you."

"Love is a losing game. All love ends up in pain. If you don't believe me, then you just don't know."

"Why you say that? Zola, you ain't but seventeen. You got a lot of life to live. You got a lot of time to let love end up in love."

"I see stuff," she said, looking out into the night. "I see it in the water. I see it in my dreams. Anytime I ever thought somebody might love me, they didn't. Or they couldn't. It ain't always their fault. Sometimes they're just being what they are."

"I love you Zola. That's gotta count for something."

Zola didn't say it back. Not that night or any other. But I never expected her to. Love is that word everyone knows but no one knows how to define. It's a feeling and a mood and an act and an energy all wrapped up in one. A multitude of adorations masquerades as love. Lust wears its shoes, infatuation puts on its lipstick, prances around in its lingerie. Manipulation, control, conceit...they all look like love sometimes. I imagine it was one of those or all of them that found their place within James Curry because less than a month after he met Zola and me, he was buying two train tickets to New York and carting her off with him.

I was on our porch shelling peas when she told me.

"We're getting married. He loves me."

"Are you sure? I mean, New York is so far away."

"What do you mean, Irene? Yes, I'm sure. James Curry is the first man I ever met that treats me like a person. And you said yourself, not thirty moons ago, that it's about time I let somebody love me."

"I just don't understand why he gotta love you in New York. Why can't he love you right here?"

"Ain't no life in the South. Everybody knows that. He has a cousin up there that has a job for him. And he says I can find work too."

"Doing what? Zola, you ain't got no skills but picking cotton and trimming sugarcane."

"Don't do that. You jealous?"

"Why would I be jealous? You don't do anything but make bad decisions. You act without thinking. You don't give two cents about anyone but yourself. And half this town says you got the devil in you. You can't even read. Who's jealous of that?"

She slapped me. Hard. Then we fought, knocking my bowl of peas to the ground and leaving each other sore and bruised, me more than her.

A week later, she was gone. I tried to make amends before she left, swallowing my pride after a night of restless sleep. At the first sign of sun, I raced to her house on Scarlett street and banged on her front door, hoping to hold her one more time, but her mama said she was already gone.

"She said she'd write," was all her mama told me.

And she did, once or twice, but then I guess life got the best of both of us.

I missed her terribly in the first year she was gone. I thought about her and James often. Were they happy? Did he peel back her hardened layers and find the tender flesh beneath? Did she find in him a love that stayed? It was easier for me to imagine that she did and I was both amused and then saddened at the thought that I didn't get to have that side of her.

But, I was one of the lucky ones. I finished school through the twelfth grade and became a schoolteacher in the same school I attended as a child, the building now painted over and slightly renovated. By 1940, Gabe Smith had asked my Daddy for my hand in marriage, proving Zola all wrong. He didn't make me wait all day, just until the time was right and the stars aligned. I almost lost him in '41 when he fell off a freight truck and broke two ribs and his right arm. He was laid up in the hospital during the worst two months of my life, which also happened to be the time when Roosevelt called a draft of all able-bodied men between the ages of 21 and 45 to register for the military. World War II was brewing, and if it weren't for Gabe's broken body, painful as it was, he would have left me altogether. Looking back at the sequence of events and divine timing, we were lucky.

Eventually, he came home and regained his strength. I took care of us with the money I made at the schoolhouse, and Mommy and Daddy helped us when they could. He was good to me. We made love almost daily, prayed before and after the act, and after my first baby was born, a chubby baldheaded girl, Gabe asked me to quit teaching for good. He wanted me all to himself, and our baby girl and I didn't mind it one bit.

By 1958, I had two more babies just like the first one, a trio of girls, each one born looking just like the last. The day after my smallest turned one, I heard the news. Gabe came in from the rig waving the *Georgia Gazette* talkin bout somebody stabbed that preacher who was leading and organizing Black folks out in Alabama. Turned out he was at a book signing in New York City, and a mentally ill Black woman named Izola Curry nearly killed him when she stabbed him in the chest. I read the paper over when Gabe handed it to me and assumed it couldn't be my Zola, but then I saw her picture, the sequined cat-eye frames, solemn frown, and the same cold eyes planted in her face ever since the dead baby. She looked older, fuller figure, rounder hips, but yet, she looked the same, a face that could belong to no other. I was nursing my baby girl in our wooden rocker, the paper draped over my lap, when my bottom lip dropped open.

Gabe was untying his boots and carrying on about the preacher and how everybody wanted him dead ever since the bus boycott so an incident like this was expected but he just didn't think they would use a Black woman to do it.

"They say that woman stabbed him deep, and that damn blade almost caught an artery. Missed it by a hair. If he'd sneezed, he'd be dead. Damn, that boy was lucky."

"It's Zola, " I whispered.

"What? What chu say?"

"Zola. Izola Ware. You remember. My best friend from right here in Savannah. They say she stabbed him."

"Oh, Zola. Can't be Zola. Lemme see that," he said, getting up and snatching the paper.

It couldn't be Zola, but it was. They say she was arrested and charged and would await trial. The preacher lived. I didn't sleep that first night or the night after wondering if Zola would. I followed the story as much as I could over the next few days until one night after supper, I was clearing our dishes away and looked up at Gabe still seated at the table.

"I want to go and see her."

It took me almost a month of begging and another month of saving before Gabe bought me a train ticket and kissed me goodbye for a little while. I left my babies in the hands of my mother, packed two sandwiches and a bag of peaches in my luggage, and spent the next two days on a train praying I would find my childhood friend still in one piece and just maybe I could love her one more time when no one else did.

The train was crowded, a sea of people. More people than I ever did see in such a small narrow space. In the colored car, a white conductor lifted my bag onto the rack overhead.

"Thank you, sir," I said quietly.

"You're most welcome. Take your seat. We're departing."

I thought I should sleep, but my mind was busy. I had never been outside Georgia before. The vision outside my window was a sight to behold. First endless fields, then clouds and barren earth. More fields. Poppy fields. Cotton fields. Sunflower fields. Then nothingness for a while. Then nighttime come.

I slept in small increments, waking with Zola on my mind. All the papers said she was a monster, deranged and soulless. Black folk said she was teeming with a legion of demons just like the ones in the Bible, and they'd need an exorcist to rid her of them, but I imagined her the same skinny girl with big breasts that she had been at seventeen.

The sky lit up like a fusion of colors on a painter's canvas. A royal blue. Yellow. A crimson red. All the shades of purple.

I heard a chatter of noise in the next car up and smelled sausage and eggs wafting down from the dining car. I stayed put, ate a peach, laid my head back and dreamt I was eleven again, sitting with Zola at the talking creek.

I woke. Outside my window, it was grey. Concrete roads and tall buildings in the distance. Gravel all around, dead train tracks. A freight train whizzed by. I fell back asleep.

I took the train all the way north past New York City to Poughkeepsie, where they were keeping my girl. I found the name of a tiny motel outside the town in the Green Book and settled there to rest my eyes for the night and then rode a bus and walked a mile in the November cool to the Matteawan State Mental Institution early the next morning.

It was a wide building clad in red brick. Looked to me like a dungeon, surrounded on all sides by a tall wired fence, and I wasn't sure if the fence was there to keep the infirm in or the right-minded out.

The sky was clear, the air a loose flavor of mountains, sweetness of cardamom and dying weeds. An uneven cobblestone road led to wide iron gates, elaborate in design, musical notes molded into its frame. I walked in, my purse carrying the peaches strewn over one shoulder, to see two guards dressed in grey, shiny metal badges adorned their chests, batons holstered in their waistbands. The shorter guard had kind eyes. He offered me a clipboard where I signed my name in neat letters. The tall one investigated my bag and removed the peaches.

"It's not allowed," he said sternly. "You can pick them up on your way out."

We waited, myself and two other visitors, in a holding room bright with white cinder block walls. Soft singing, a roar of shrieks, and painful groans rang out through the corridors. I felt scared and wondered if Zola was among the voices.

When I went in to her, she was sitting in a chair to the side of the bed, by the window, a small window that let in little light and faced a brick wall. I called to her and she turned but didn't seem to register my face. I suppose I looked different too, heavier after three babies. I went to her side, dropped my purse on the floor, and grabbed her hand, hesitant.

She didn't flinch but kept her gaze on me. She wore the cat eyeglasses that covered fatigued eyes, deep set and empty, her hair pinned back in a chignon, her thick frame covered in a dingy hospital gown. It smelled of soiled laundry and urine that someone had tried to scrub clean with peroxide but didn't finish the job.

"Do you remember me?" I asked her.

She stared.

"I'm Reenie," I said.

In my memory, I like to think she smiled, but I know better. Zola never smiled, even in our younger years, so it wouldn't make sense for her to do it then. But her demeanor changed at the mention of my name. Her eyes recognized me. I sat back on the bed, extending her hand, still in mine. Then I smiled. "Hi."

"Reenie." She used her other hand to point and shake her finger at me, jogging her own memory. "What are you doing here?"

I chuckled to hear her speak. "I heard you were in some trouble."

"Ain't I always?"

"Yeah. Far as I can remember, you are."

We sat that way for a while. I caught her up on Gabe and my girls. I asked her about James. She said they split years ago, but she kept his name. I told her I was sorry. She said don't be. She was working as a domestic and renting an apartment in Harlem. I opened my bag and saw a lone peach the guard had missed. I grabbed it and handed it to Zola. For a short while, it felt like old times, even down to my hesitation when I wanted to ask her the hard question.

"Zola, what happened? Did you stab that man?"

She shrugged her shoulders and took a bite. "Sometimes things have to happen, and if ain't nobody else around to do it, then you the one to do it."

"Zola, what are you talking about? Why did you have to do that? They say you're in a lot of trouble. They say you're not well."

She swallowed. "Maybe I'm the well one and it's everybody else who's sick."

Zola always talked in riddles that I never did understand, but that's why I loved her so much, because I knew they made sense to her.

"I love you Zola. I never stopped loving you. I never stopped thinking of you. I worry for you. Maybe when you get outta here, you come back down to Georgia. Me and Gabe, we can take care of you."

"Take care of me? What makes you think I need care?"

I shrugged. "I dunno. I don't like the thought of you up here all by yourself."

Zola rolled a bite around in her mouth. "Is that creek still down there? Remember? The magic one that speaks."

I smiled, remembering. "Don't you miss that place?"

"Only place it seemed the world couldn't get to us. Only place we could talk and no one would know our secrets."

Zola turned her chair and faced the window and the brick wall, directing her words there. "I used to think it was the creek that was doing all the talking, but maybe not. You believe in God, Reenie?"

"What chu asking?"

Zola set her pit holding hand in her lap and let the half-eaten peach roll to the floor.

"You ever think some people are better off dead?" she asked the wall. "Like all those folks that died in Hiroshima. Women and even babies. Maybe them dying was the better option. Better than whatever they had to endure while they was livin. I think about that. I think about how much better off I'd be if somebody would have killed me before my daddy had the chance to ruin me. Cuz he sure ruined me. He sure planted something in me along with his seed, spoiled jizz that infected my soul and birthed a whole host of spirits that won't leave me alone."

"Zola, what chu saying?" I whispered.

"I'm just saying I see things, Reenie. The preacher man, I saw him in my dreams or a vision or a moment of clarity, and the years in front of him ain't got nothing good for him. Just a whole lot of pain and brokenness and little babies without a daddy. A woman without a lover, that's what he'll leave behind."

"Zola?"

"I'm saying, sometimes we too smart, too holy, too altruistic to see the good. We can't see the forest cuz all them trees in the way. Preacher man better off dead, by my own hand than the devil's. I cut him with love, saving him from all the devils up ahead that would kill him with hate. That's a kind of hell I wouldn't wish on nobody. Ain't nothin coming but babies growing up with a dead daddy. I failed at what I was trying to do. I aimed to kill and I failed, but if I would've won, those babies still just sleeping eggs in the mother's womb...they would've been the lucky ones. I wasn't trying to hurt him. I was trying to save him."

"They say that man ain't doing nothing but good though. He's acting out of love."

She turned and met my eyes. "Love is a losing game Reenie. All love ends up in pain."

I didn't get Zola. Not then, but I do now. Fortune is relative, and how do we measure the absence of pain?

I left her after a long afternoon expecting to see her again. I would go back to visit when they were ready to let her go, and she would live with Gabe and me, maybe meet another love, one that stayed. Maybe have some babies, but probably not. She was already up in age.

I rode back to Savannah planning a life for her, for us, hoping to salvage something of the way things used to be. There is something incredibly enchanting about keeping someone in your life who knew you when you were young. I wanted to save her from the rocks the world was throwing the way she saved me from little ugly Memphis Black so many years before. I wanted my girls to grow up knowing their Auntie Zola and what a fine friend she was to me.

None of that ever happened. The years rolled on and my letters to Zola were never answered. The newspapers said she wasn't well enough to stand trial and would spend the rest of her life in that institution. The preacher died anyway some years later. It was just as Zola said, an assassination, an execution by the ones that never wanted us to win, and he was survived by four young children and a widow.

Gabe and I drove to New York City in '75 and made plans to visit Zola, but they said she was moved and couldn't tell us where. It was like she never even existed, a black dot in a vast ocean, never seen, never known. I heard both her parents died years before and her siblings were off living their lives in different corners of the world. I tracked down James Curry, the man that stole her away from me, and he was living in California with a wife and four grown boys. She never had any children to mourn her absence. The lucky bastards. Zola was gone, a mist that almost never was. She remained a nearly forgotten parenthesis in my life for many years until this morning.

Gabe had died in '98 from a tumor in his brain and an infection in his legs. The first two years after his death were the hardest. There were many lonely nights where my heart was brought very low, and I desired death more than I did life. I toyed with the idea of suicide. A hanging, a falling, an easy death with liquor and sleeping pills where I could drift off on a cloud. But I thought of my children, although grown, having to live with the memory that their mother left by choice.

Perhaps then, it was my own children who saved me, unbeknownst to them, and for what, I am still unsure. But if it were not for them, I for certain would have no guilt for the thing I wanted most to do. So then, I was stuck here, held captive in chains, by my own guilty conscience.

Having no children, and thus no guilt, Zola was the free one.

Zola was lucky. And yet, even in her condition, a continual and perpetual existence underwater, she stayed.

It was this revelation that jolted me from the slumber I had been in from the day Gabe swallowed his last breath and stirred me to sit upright again. I moved to New Jersey to live with my granddaughter, Patricia, who has cared for me boldly.

And now, Zola is dead. People age, and then they die. My own death is likely to follow, and in these moments, I see all of life as a vapor, moving quickly and without notice, and know now the nostalgia my mother felt when I wouldn't stop growing.

# Laundering

Wesley's eyes were small and wet. The tear paths etched into her cheeks complemented the roundness of them. The washing machines in her peripheral vision droned on, a cacophony of noise. The iridescence of the hanging white lights was unrelenting. The sight caused Wesley to involuntarily retreat further into the uncomfortable metal seat she occupied. Her back ached. She laid her head on the small, foldable table, bringing her arms up as shields to block out the light and noise. The rustling of her raincoat annoyed her, and she regretted putting it on despite the downpour outside.

The small, beige cinderblock room was mostly empty now, save for the occasional patron that slugged in, damp from the evening's deluge, with a discolored sack of clothes and pockets singing with the sound of dirty, loose coins. The stinging stench of bleach and the hovering stink of artificial fragrances emanating from strewn detergent bottles only added to the smog of the poorly ventilated room, causing Wesley's ever-growing discomfort to worsen. This place had been her cell for months now. She thought she would've become desensitized to it. But with every passing shift, she felt more agitated by the sights, smells, and sounds. Mostly, she felt more stuck.

"Can I get change for this twenty," a middle-aged woman said in a way that was not so much a question, but an order. She, hair up in a bonnet, was dressed in gray house slippers despite the weather, and a matching black sweatsuit that reeked of smoke.

Wesley gingerly took the wet bill from the woman's creased hands. The woman watched her instinctively, her eyes meeting Wesley's sullen gaze more than Wesley appreciated.

"What's the matter with you, child?" the woman asked, as Wesley counted out eighty quarters.

"Nothin'." She almost losing count. The cold metal felt foreign on her damp palms. "Here."

The woman grabbed the small, white bag with the *Young's Suds* logo printed in bright blue letters accompanied by rainbow-gradient bubbles. She eyed Wesley once more, deciding whether she wanted to be nosy or give it rest. She chose the latter. It was a rainy Friday night. She didn't have time for kids who weren't her own anyway.

"You're too pretty to be doin' all that frownin' child. Tell that handsome father of yours that Tiffany said 'hello'," she stated, the edge of her swollen lips twinging upwards. She walked back to her machine.

Wesley inhaled, exhaled, and slunk further into her seat.

*That* was something Wesley was used to by now. Many women, both young and old in town, throwing themselves at her father. It was less about his appearance and more about his pocketbook. Locally, he was something of a blip in the system. A successful Black businessman in the South. An oxymoron. He somehow went from growing up in Section 8 to being the one who owned the rentals. He loved to yap about how he took night classes so he could work during the day, seven days a week, cleaning buildings. He was proud of the struggle, and he wanted people to know it. Women were drawn to his success, or the appearance thereof. No one knew about the second mortgage he had taken out on the house or the phone calls from collections that Wesley knew not to answer.

Going anywhere was a chore as Wesley was a mirror image of him. People liked to joke that instead of receiving half her DNA from each parent, Wesley had budded from her father. Those comments always made her uncomfortable. She wanted to be as far removed from her father as possible, but that was difficult to do when his face was always the one people saw when looking at her. She was him. She worked *for* him. Had to. She had even been named after him.

*That's so cute. Weston and Wesley. Precious.* This was the usual reaction to the realization that the prominent father-daughter duo of Sehon County was named Weston and Wesley Young.

Wesley thought it was possessive, another way for him to dictate her choices while not even being present.

The small chime of the front doorbell brought her out of her stupor. The figure that walked in was a young guy, early twenties with a buzz cut and damp jeans. His face was structured and pleasant. Yet, Wesley noticed a small mark on the right side of his forehead that broke up the smoothness. The mark resembled a coffee stain, oblong and dark. His skin was lighter than her own, but still not what others would consider 'light-skinned.' He carried a black umbrella and a khaki-colored bag stuffed to the brim.

Just as he sauntered over to the washing machine directly to his right, the rain began pelting the windows like mini pebbles being thrown. At that point, Wesley wished her father would install speakers in the place. *Enjoy the sound of community, Wes*--he'd said. The only sounds of community Wesley had become accustomed to were the clothes tumbling, coins jingling, small children screaming, and machines squeaking. Right now though, everything was quiet besides the growing tempest outside and the two patrons.

"Uh, I think this one's broken," a voice materialized from out of the air.

Her eyes picked up and met those of the young man's. She hadn't recognized him when he'd walked in. His hair had been longer then, able to hide the birthmark that was now easily visible. He was bold for walking through the doors. Or stupid.

"Louis," she said, disregarding his statement.

"Hey," was the extent of his reply.

"Hi."

The last time she'd seen him was late January before all the police tape had cleared and people slowly began whispering about other gossip, becoming bored with no further developments. Her father had been glad that the hot water had stopped boiling and had settled at a low simmer. Wesley didn't think about the situation anymore if she could help it. She just knew that it had, for all intents and purposes, ruined her life.

He ambled over to the opposite side of the washers, dragging his khaki sack behind him. He glanced at her momentarily, then busied himself with filling three machines.

Wesley stared reluctantly, eyes holding his effortless routine. He pressed *start* on all of the machines, one after the other. The front-loading washing machines held tsunamis of suds and clothes that Wesley wished she could lose herself in. He made his way over to her, hands in pockets. Wesley suddenly became acutely aware of what she looked like: gray rain boots that squeaked with every nervous motion, dark wash overalls with a senior class t-shirt, and a navy raincoat. Her braids were pulled back in a loose ponytail. She immediately wanted to not be there more than ever.

"You always look so bummed nowadays?" he asked, as he brought a plastic chair up to the small foldable table that held the cashbox, rolls of change, and her cell phone that was currently off to dissuade her father from checking in on her every hour. A 12-hour shift became a little more bearable with the absence of her father.

"No," Wesley answered, uncertain how this conversation was going to play out.

He sat down.

He looked the same as he had back at the beginning of the year—besides the haircut—when night and day seemed to switch places, when night came on quick and absolute. "Well, if I remember right, you had this same look about you the last time I saw you."

His round lips pressed together firmly but rose slightly in a smirk.

"If I remember right," Wesley mimicked, "the last time I saw you, you fucked up my life so..."

The end of her statement hung in the air and charged the short distance between them. The middle-aged woman had been staring at them for some time, and at the sound of Wesley cursing, she raised an eyebrow, now deeply invested. She noticeably slowed down folding her whites.

Louis' hand rubbed his shaved head, nervously. Suddenly, Wesley felt tired.

"Yeah...about that...I'm real sorry, Wes."

Her tiredness turned to nausea. She pushed her chair back into the wall of frozen memories. The black-framed photos of her father in various suits standing in front of the properties he owned around the county. The one in the middle was of him in front of the building they were sitting in, on opening day, comically—oversized scissors in hand. That had been years ago, before all the fissures.

"What do you expect me to say to that?"

"I don't know."

"Okay, then." Wesley stood up, grabbed the broom from the corner, and began to sweep the floor she had already cleaned twice before. "Where the hell did you even go?"

"The East Coast," he replied. "That was always the plan. Remember?"

Wesley pretended to be interested in the small dust pile she'd created. How more dust had managed to accumulate since she last swept was beyond her. She turned, back pointed away from Louis.

***

January's air was electrifying, all cold and heavy in her nostrils. Walking through the door of her brown-bricked home, the icy ground crunching beneath her, she lumbered down the desolate road and into the black truck that was idling by the corner stop sign. She remembered watching the jolly Santa Claus wave its animatronic arm back and forth rigidly, eyes dead. Next to him in her yard was a gaggle of multicolored elves holding an assortment of presents. The dark inside of the vehicle lit up in a mosaic of color as the hedge lights shone brightly in the late-night air. It was already the second week of January, and her house still looked like a Christmas catalog, thanks to her father.

"Did you get it?" Louis' voice broke the silence.

His facial expression was hard to decipher. He wore a slight smile, but his bushy brows were furrowed. His hair had been longer then, braided down in cornrows. She loved it. He was dressed in a simple outfit: dark gray sweatpants, a plain black top, and a simple denim jacket, despite the frigid temperature. He was wearing his glasses, Wesley had noticed. He only wore those when he wanted to be able to really focus.

"Yeah," she replied. She hadn't realized until that moment that her heart had been beating. Now, she worried he could hear it. As if he could read her mind, he placed a hand on her knee and squeezed it faintly, in reassurance. She pulled out a neatly wrapped stack of hundreds from her black puffer jacket and placed it on the dash. Both stared at it. Each for different reasons.

He saw it as a plane ride, a new life, revenge. She saw an act of defiance, but her apprehension had made it so this act had taken more than a week to carry out and over two months of convincing. She had finally agreed to it when Louis promised he'd take her with him.

She didn't know what to expect, but she wanted to leave before she was stuck permanently.

She used to talk about college with her mom on nights when her father's absence was heavier than usual. At that time, only a small child, the thought of being grown was unfathomable. Wesley regarded college daydreams as another aspect of make-believe. Her mom would whisper capitals of states into her small ears as they laid together on the couch, staring at the revolving ceiling fan. Places they would travel. Things they would do. Schools she could attend.

"Boston is by the sea," her mother said. "We could go sailing."

Wesley, in her pajamas underneath a heavy gray comforter, replied, "I can't swim, Mommy."

"I'll teach ya." Her mother grabbed her daughter, bringing her closer to her chest.

"What about Daddy?" Wesley asked, balancing precariously on the edge of sleep.

"Just us girls."

Wesley nodded and fell asleep, only waking when her dad came through the door at much too late an hour for him to have just been at the office. Infidelity reeked on him, but Wesley only knew that her father smelled sweet. Like cherry candies somedays. Other days vanilla. She often wondered why her mom would get so upset with him when he smelled so lovely. It wasn't until she was older, and she had caught her mother crying in the laundry room, did she realize that the sweetness was wrong.

"Is this everything?" Louis asked, flipping through the stack, entranced.

"I think so," she replied, hands in her lap. "I tried to count it like three times. But I didn't want to be in the cellar too long or he'd start asking for me. It should be five grand, though."

Louis let out what Wesley could only think of as a snort of joy. He pulled one of the hundreds out, crisp as ever, and smelled it.

Wesley laughed at his ridiculous behavior. She never cared for money like Louis did. She figured it was because her father had always had it in some form or fashion because he was good at making deals. Louis, on the other hand, grew up much differently.

She relaxed a bit. There was no sign of movement from the house and no indication that her father had woken up when she left through the front door. She had practiced how to disable the alarm system four times that week. It took her 'cleaning' his office seven times to even find the code.

"I can't believe you did it," Louis said, eyes still glued to the stack in his hands.

Wesley nodded to herself. She had done it because her father deserved it, she told herself.

"He's a lyin' son of a bitch," she heard Louis say under his breath. The anger in his voice was easy to hear. It was Wesley's turn this time to offer a reassuring squeeze.

"We're gonna do it," she said, trying to convince herself as well.

They had concocted a plan in late November, five months after Louis had begun doing yard work for Weston Young's properties. Wesley, eighteen and in need of a summer job, had reluctantly agreed to be her father's secretary of sorts. Answer the phone. Take messages. Organize his desk. All the things she did at home for free. It was there at her father's Activity Center she'd run into Louis, all tall and glistening in the humid summer sun.

"Stay away from him," her father told her one afternoon after catching her staring at Louis clipping bushes. "His people aren't good people."

The comment almost made her laugh aloud, but she knew better than to do that. She nodded in obedience. Her father strolled away to tend to whatever he did during the day. Wesley really had no firm idea. He moved around the county, from property to property, cell phone always in hand. Since her mother left, he seemed to compensate by making dicey business decisions.

One morning Louis walked up to her, the look of a mad man on his face.

"Where's your father?" he screamed, eyes wild.

The sudden outburst in the unopened center had made Wesley jump. It was only seven in the morning.

"He left two days ago on a trip or something," she answered, confused. She had only spoken to Louis a handful of times over the summer. But since it was November, they were both back in school, so she rarely ever saw him. However, that handful let her know that his demeanor was usually nonchalant.

"The hell he did." He walked around the small station that Wesley had converted into a secretarial space and pounded on the brown door that had *Weston Young* engraved on it.

"What's wrong with you?" Wesley asked, wondering if she should call somebody.

Louis, still fuming, turned toward her.

"Your father is fucking my mother." His voice broke toward the end.

Wesley didn't know what she had expected him to say but hearing that made her sick. "How...when..."

"Walked into our spare room last night because I thought I heard something. Turned out, it was Mr. Young and my mom."

Silence.

Wesley sat back down. She had known her father was licentious. Her mother left years ago, after the fifth woman came forward. Wesley always wondered why her mother hadn't taken her too, like they had always planned. It had happened while Wesley was in school. Her mother had walked her to school that day, the entire way, which was unusual for her to do because she was usually in a hurry to get to the nursing home for her shift. Yet that day, her mother's smooth hand held Wesley's all the way to the school grounds. Nothing else had been off about that morning. Nothing hinted at the screams from the previous night after the phone call that shattered the illusion. Her mother had handed over the brown paper lunch bag and looked into her daughter's unwitting eyes. Wesley hugged her mother, happy that she had company. Her mom rubbed her back, as she did when they laid on the couch. She told her child she loved her and would see her later. That was the only time Wesley could think of that her mother had lied to her.

After a while, Wesley decided that she was left because of her name and her face. She was a constant reminder of her father.

After her mother left, they had moved to Sehon County, about three hours away from where she grew up. She had tried to forgive him for making her motherless, but the steady rotation of women, some married, erased any chances of that. The only reason she played nice was because he was her financial support. She needed him to pay for college. And her father was smart; he didn't dip his toe in the female pool of this town. No, he waded in the waters of nearby counties careful not to stay in any one area too long. Until Louis' mother.

The plan was simple. Steal the money. Expose her father. Leave town. Find her mother. The first step had surprisingly gone off without hiccups. It was the exposing part that had proved their undoing.

Louis' mom had been in an entanglement with Wesley's father for a while. She had even gotten pregnant. Louis learned this after interrogating her after Mr. Young fled their house. Louis' dad, embarrassed and intimidated, left without confrontation. The crazy thing was that Louis' mom hadn't cared. She wanted to be with Wesley's father and that had made everything more complicated.

There was one thing on their side: Mr. Young loved women, but he loved himself and his reputation more. He would do anything to keep it untainted. Even dump his pregnant mistress. If he wanted to run for selectman, which he intended to do the following election season, he couldn't have the mess.

He wrote a check and told her to take care of it.

Louis had convinced her otherwise. They needed proof, and the baby would be it.

The last time they had seen each other was in January after the money handoff. Louis' mother went to stay with his grandmother. The plan was to do a DNA test and send that to the paper, while also posting anonymous messages on Facebook from women her father had wronged in the past. However, her father was a seasoned veteran in the roulette of sex and money. The stolen money was quickly noticed. Wesley hadn't known that he installed cameras in the cellar. It made sense, though. A man with a lot of skeletons had to be paranoid. Everything crumbled after that. His own daughter was on the surveillance video. This saved her—kind of. He didn't need that information getting out. So instead, he gave her an ultimatum: return the money or he would report Louis to the authorities. The former wasn't an option as Louis had spent the money on plane tickets and a security deposit on an apartment across the country.

She remembered when it happened. The flashing lights. The absurd number of cop cars. Everything happened all at once. She tried to warn and convince him that they had to leave right then. Instead of listening, fury led him to the Activity Center, baseball bat in hand. As the vehicles arrived, Louis had already bolted into the woods. The sound of breaking windows stayed with Wesley for weeks after.

Another chime of the door broke the reel that was playing in Wesley's head. She hadn't realized it, but she had started crying again. She quickly rubbed the tears into her skin and made her way back to her seat. The chime brought in another soggy patron with two duffel bags and a small child with bright red rain boots who definitely shouldn't have been out in this weather.

"You shouldn't be here," Wesley finally spoke. She had found herself thinking about him less and less as the days rolled into one another. She had decided to be grateful for that. After it all went down, her chest felt like it was seconds away from caving. He left without her. Just like her mother had done.

"You shouldn't either," he replied. He looked sad, like a child who just lost his favorite toy.

"Well, you kind of ruined that chance for me. I'm stuck here, paying off my debt to my father for the money you had me steal. He said, 'Five grand is a semester of college,' and that I couldn't go because I chose to spend the money on a boy and extortion. Knowing him, he won't let me go next semester either."

The small child, red rain boots squeaking, ran up to the table, almost slipping in the process. She held up a smushed ten dollar bill, looking up at Wesley with big, curious eyes. A small smile flashed across Wesley's face as she counted out the coins, placing them in the small open hands of the freckled child.

The child's eyes swelled with gratitude for being entrusted with such a prize.

"Thankyamaam," she uttered, words bleeding into each other from excitement. She dashed back to her mother in a half-skip, half-run.

Wesley realized that she had never put out the wet floor sign.

Just then, three buzzers sounded one after the other after the other. Wesley looked at the washers and back at her old accomplice.

"Your machines stopped," she said.

He shook his head.

"Wes," he began, "I came here to apologize."

"I heard you." Wesley grabbed her phone and turned it on. Anything to distract herself from this. "Just go."

Louis stood, hesitated for a moment, then walked back to his machines. He didn't bother loading his wet clothes into dryers. He knew his time was up. He packed them in his khaki sack, making the outside a darker shade. He slung the bag over his shoulder and walked back over to Wesley.

"Here." He placed a small picture in front of her—a swaddled child in the arms of Louis' mother. Wesley did not move.

"I'm only here till tomorrow. I came back to see her." He gestured toward the photo. "They stay upstate with my grandma."

Louis rocked back and forth on his heels for a second or two. Then he walked to the door, pushed it open, and was gone with the piercing ring of the bell.

Wesley sat there, stunned. She slowly moved her long fingers toward the photo, turning it over to give herself a moment to breathe. There, penciled on the back, was his name and a phone number.

Underneath that was her name, 'Wes,' and the details for a one-way ride out of Sehon County.

# tongue: tied and twisted

It feels screamy in my head.

The therapist frowns, and maybe hums a little. "What do you mean by that?"

What the fuck? I mean what I said. "I don't know. Just, it's loud in my head. Like screaming."

"But is that a feeling?"

If I feel it, it's a feeling, right? But I just sigh. "I guess I feel anxious."

I don't feel anxious. I feel screamy.

Her blue eyes light up behind her oversized hipster glasses. "Well, what do you think is causing that?"

I don't fucking know. Life? What's supposed to be causing it? I take a deep breath and look at my watch. Ten more minutes. "Actually, I need to leave a little early today. I have an appointment."

"At 8 PM?"

"It was the only time I could get a grocery delivery. I don't want it sitting out for too long. I mean, it's ten minutes." It's my ten minutes. She gets paid either way. I stand to go.

"Spend some time thinking about what's causing your anxiety. Maybe try some deep breathing."

Yeah. Maybe.

***

"I wonder if it's because I'm Black."

"If what's because you're Black?"

"That Jodi left. That she doesn't care how I feel. That she thinks I don't have feelings."

"What makes you say that? She knows you have feelings."

"Does she? We were together for nine years, and she literally said that she had to leave because staying would hurt her new girlfriend's feelings. What about my feelings? She barely knows that girl."

"Well, she knows you have feelings."

"She obviously doesn't care about them."

"Isn't it better to know that now?"

"No. It'd be better for her to fucking care."

"Why are you so angry?"

"I'm allowed to be angry. Why shouldn't I be angry?"

"Sometimes anger masks other feelings. Sometimes anger overwhelms other people."

Is this chick scared of me? She's got seven inches and at least fifty pounds on me. That's me being nice about her weight. I am not a scary person. I am five foot two in heels.

I look at my watch.

I feel sad and abandoned, and lonely, and yes, I feel angry.

***

I'm moving my Grand-mere's recipe book when a card falls to the floor. A recipe for tongue. I don't remember her ever making tongue. I tuck the card back in the book. I should probably just throw it away. Who makes tongue?

A boyfriend in college took me to his abuela's for lengua tacos. I remember her staring at me, watching me eat it. Was that a test, or did she just hope I'd like it? It was fine. Not great. A little chewy. In the car, he made a face. "Fucking lengua? I'm sorry. I don't know what's wrong with her. Nasty."

I assured him it was fine.

He broke up with me a few weeks later. About something else, obviously. But I always wondered if I maybe wasn't supposed to like the lengua.

***

Grand-mere's family is not French, or even Creole. They're not from Louisiana or the islands. She just thought it sounded better than "grandma." She doesn't practice voodoo or believe in magic. In fact, her and Grandpa were both raised in the kind of Pentecostal church where you aren't even allowed to celebrate Halloween. There are pictures of Grandpa's dad dressed in a sharp suit, maybe thirteen years old, with a snake wrapped around his neck, in front of a whole tent full of white people. What did all those white people think about that little boy playing with a copperhead snake?

"Juliette!" The white guy from accounting always calls me Juliette. "My name's Joanna."

"I know. But I grew up with a Black girl named Juliette."

"I grew up with a girl named Juliette too. She was Greek."

He laughs.

\*\*\*

"Well, did he like this Juliette?" the therapist asks.

What difference does it make? I'm frowning too hard to speak.

"Maybe you should ask. Maybe it's a term of endearment."

"We work together. Are we supposed to be endearing?"

"Well, I suppose you could report it. If it bothers you that much."

Yes. I suppose I could.

\*\*\*

I slip on a piece of paper on the kitchen floor. I don't fall, but damn. I put that stupid tongue recipe back in the book.

\*\*\*

It's screamy in my head again.

Jody's text says her new girlfriend is too demanding.

Am I supposed to care? Am I supposed to answer?

"That sucks," I say.

What did she expect?

"I didn't realize you wanted a serious relationship," she'd said as she packed her stuff.

"We've been together nine years."

"I don't know if I want that kind of relationship," she said as she packed her stuff to move in with someone she'd known for six months.

"Then why are you moving in with someone?"

She doesn't seem to understand the irony, or whatever.

I go to the garage to cry.

\*\*\*

"I've always admired Black women," the therapist says. She was highly recommended by several women I work with. White women I work with. "It's hard when everyone expects you to be weak and stupid."

"It's hard when people don't expect you to be human."

"I just mean, at least the standard you're expect to uphold is positive."

"Is it? I'm a person. I have feelings. I need protection, and safety, and love. I'm not just here to give those things to other people."

"You sound angry."

Do I now?

***

There are four Black therapists in this city. How many people live here? I look it up. Seven hundred thousand. And four Black therapists. That's not fair. There are seven Black therapists, but three don't take my insurance. So they don't count.

Cecile is my preferred. Her bio says she works with racialized trauma, and diagnoses adult autism. My ex asked once if I might be autistic because I cried "inappropriately" at a Disney cartoon. Cecile is not taking new patients.

Susan is taking new patients, but doesn't take appointments in the evenings. I know for a fact that two of my coworkers take long lunches weekly for therapy, but when I asked my supervisor, she said I'd have to get permission from HR, and really, why can't I just do it after work? I asked my coworkers if they had to get permission from HR. They look confused at the question.

Michael and Jamilah are married. Their bios don't say that, but their offices are at the same residential address. And her bio says "spirituality," but his specifically says "Jesus." Good God no. I might trust my soul to a snake handling preacher, but not my mind.

My current therapist was highly recommended by several of my coworkers.

***

What's that piece of paper on the living room floor? One good thing about Jodi leaving is that I can keep things as clean as I want. No laundry on the dining table. No rogue papers on the floor.

"I don't want to make this fucking tongue, Grand-mere," I say to the ether.

***

The meat counter at the Mexican market always smells too meaty. Like they actually butcher animals there. Bloody. I prefer the sterility of the natural market. But I'm standing here, smelling the blood, and I wonder if the natural market smells unnaturally clean. I barely cook anyway. And I'm here because I'm cheap. The natural market only had frozen tongue, and wanted an arm and a leg for it. It's cast off. I know that. I'm not paying the same for tongue as I do for rib eye. Especially if it's frozen.

One of the tongues in the case is smaller than the others. I point to it. My mind goes blank, looking for the Spanish. "Poquito," I say.

The butcher laughs a little, and wraps up the smallest tongue in waxed paper, slaps on the sticker. "Need anything else?" he asks with a softly southern accent like everyone else around here.

"No. Thanks."

He salutes me. "See you next time."

I walk away and realize I should've asked him what the hell I'm supposed to do with this thing now. The recipe keeps showing up, but I never read it the whole way through. So I stopped at the market on my way home from work, but I don't know what else I need. I don't really cook much. Jodi liked to eat out. It hasn't been long enough since we broke up for me to care about what I eat. Or if I eat.

I grab a couple of onions and some garlic. That's about all you need for anything, right?

"Lengua?" the older woman who was standing behind me at the meat counter asks.

How long have I been standing here, staring at herbs?

I nod.

"You need some lime and culantro. And salsa verde for after the cooking."

What's culantro? But it's sitting right in front of me, so I put it in my basket, even though it's obviously not in my Grand-mere's recipe.

I mean, this is someone's grandma too, by the looks of her.

"Thank you," I say, smiling. I make it a point to smile when interacting with strangers.

She smiles back. "You welcome. I hope your husband enjoys."

Yeah, me too?

***

"I see where you scratched it, but it doesn't look red to me," the dermatologist says.

That's the same thing Jodi said.

He tells me to use the number one dermatologist recommended over the counter lotion, and switch to an unscented laundry detergent. Which I did months ago. I struggle not to scratch.

He taps on his tablet and is about to dismiss me.

"I'd like a second opinion."

His mouth opens mutely like he's not sure if I understand what I said.

"I'd like to see a Black doctor," I say.

He rolls his eyes and taps away, shaking his head a little. "If you say so," he whispers.

I do say so.

"A lot of skin problems are actually anxiety. I can refer you to a therapist."

There are two Black dermatologists in this city. Neither take my insurance. I settle for Dr. Khatri. He walks into my appointment, shining in his white lab coat. His undertones are brown, where mine are yellow, but we're probably the same skin tone, absorbing the same amount of light.

"Oh dear," he says, stroking the red rash on my arm. "It's likely just eczema, but we'll take a culture, in case. Is it anywhere else?"

I point to the back of my neck.

He hums. "Try wearing your hair off your neck, or switching shampoos. If you use shampoo."

I nod. I don't use shampoo, but I rarely tell people that. "Sometimes it's on my face too. Between my eyebrows, but it's not as bad now."

"It's a little red."

He can see it?

He taps on his tablet. "Dr. B—prescribed a bleaching cream? What for? You didn't fill the prescription."

"He said I had vitiligo. But it's just a couple of little spots." I show him.

"Does it bother you? Does it grow or change?"

"No."

"This cream isn't the best for darker skin anyway. I'll discharge it?"

I nod.

"My little sister called her vitiligo 'reverse freckles'." He chuckles as he tappity taps on the tablet.

I laugh too.

"I'll prescribe a couple of things for the itching. If you don't scratch it, most people won't see it."

"Thank you."

***

It's screamy in my head again, so I don't bother going to therapy. Jodi texts and says she feels lonely and suicidal, so I ask her to call me. She doesn't. Should I be worried? I should be worried. I am worried. But also, fuck her. Maybe?

I call, and she doesn't answer.

*I'm fine*, she texts.

I think about calling the police, but that seems like a lot of work that I don't have energy for. I don't know where they live anyway.

I should cook that tongue, but now I can't find the recipe. Where'd I put it? Why am I like this?

I think about throwing it away, but that's a lot of work I don't have energy for.

***

The therapist calls me herself, so I go ahead and reschedule my appointment. Usually, she has the receptionist call.

***

I put my hair up in a puff on top of my head instead of pressing it.

"Did you cut your hair, Juliette?"

I don't even look his way.

Later that day, my supervisor calls me into her office. "Kevin says you were rude to him today."

"I don't even remember seeing him today. And no offense, but is that even a supervisor level problem? Do you really want us coming to you every time someone doesn't notice us in the copy room?"

She frowns like that hadn't occurred to her.

"May I go?"

"Of course. Sorry. I like your hair that way."

"Thank you."

I'm leaving for the day and Kevin holds the door.

"Did you cut your hair, Joanna?"

"No, just a different style."

"It looks nice. Have a nice night, Joanna."

"You too, Kevin."

***

We sit in silence for a long time. Not pleasant silence.

"Have you heard from Jodi?" the therapist asks.

I tell her about it.

"How does that make you feel?"

I hate that question. "Sad and lonely," I say.

She hums and taps her pen on her pad. "Is that all?"

Those are pretty big emotions. I don't have energy for anything else. "No. I don't think so."

"You sound angry."

Do I? "I told you I'm sad and lonely. Why do you think I'm angry?"

"You just sound angry to me."

"You're right. I just sound angry to you. I never sound anything but angry to you. Maybe that's your ears, not my sounds."

She draws back a little, her eyes wide.

I look at my watch. I've only been here fifteen minutes. "I'm gonna go."

"Excuse me?"

"I'mma go," I repeat. I pick up my bag to find my keys.

She looks at her watch. "I'm sorry. You're just usually so articulate.

"I used the words that best articulate how and feel and what I'm about to do. Are your white patients who say 'gonna' inarticulate?"

The receptionist looks up from her book as I leave the office. I was going to just walk out, but I stop.

"I'd like to cancel my next appointment."

She taps on her keyboard and asks to confirm my birth date. "Do you want to reschedule?"

"No. I won't be back."

"You might like Dr. Kiwanuka better." She hands me a card.

"Is he Japanese?"

"No." She thinks for a moment. "I know he lived in Uganda, but that's not where he's from. I can't remember. Sorry. But he's African-American. And he'll take after hours appointments as long as you keep a credit card on file."

"Thank you."

"I like your hair that way. I had to stop wearing bangs to make my eczema clear up too."

She notices me? My eczema? I don't even know her name. "Have a nice night."

***

Jodi and the therapist text me on the same day.

*Why haven't I heard from you?* Jodi says. Like she deserves to hear from me.

*I'd like to have a closing session,* the therapist says. Like she deserves to hear from me.

My brain is hella screamy.

This time, when I step on the index card, I slip. I crack my elbow on the floor. I growl, and cuss, and snatch the card off the floor. I'm looking for the book to put it away when I finally look at it.

I finally really look at it.

It's not a recipe at all.

It's a spell.

A spell? Grand-mere is not from the islands, or bayou, or anywhere else where people might use a beef tongue to make someone forget her name. Can I use it for two people? Not that I believe in that type of thing.

And since I don't really believe, it doesn't really matter that I don't have the exact list of "ingredients."

I get a candle, and the remnants of a bottle of whiskey leftover from a party, and a picture of Jodi. An appointment card from the therapist. An appointment card from Dr. B, the dermatologist, while I'm at it. I find a thick embroidery needle and black thread in Grand-mere's sewing box. I write the spells and rub the tongue down with whiskey before cutting it open. I light the candle and imagine their mouths full of cat shit and rusty nails. It's too hard to sew the tongue closed. I was never good at sewing. I wrap the spells, and picture, and the appointment cards inside the tongue with the thread. I seal the tongue shut with the candle wax. Then I wrap it in plastic for good measure. Now what? I'm supposed to nail the tongue to a tree and let it rot. I don't have a tree. I don't know where Jodi lives now, and I don't want to know. But I do know where she works. There are a lot of trees in back of the building.

I blast music and sing as I drive across town. Are there cameras in this lot? It doesn't really matter. I park, and look at my phone for a moment. I walk to the passenger side like I'm checking my tire. I fling the tongue into the copse of cedar trees sidearm like a Frisbee, and it thuds to the ground. Nothing about me itches for the first time in months.

*Hey,* I text Jodi.

*Who's this?*

I laugh.

I feel light and happy for the first time in months.

# A Woman's Place

Melody died in the body of an old lady, her wrinkled skin drooped from her cheeks, her pits, and her butt. She was only fifteen months. She was buried fast fast, sealed in a box used to store her father's new stereos. Her nanny Chikodi was returned to the village because Melody's grandmamma believed she drank her granddaughter's blood little by little until she dried up and died. Chikodi was no blood drinker, although she drank most of Melody's infant formula and cereal. Maybe her greed was a subtle form of witchcraft, maybe not. Maybe a seven-year-old nanny needed supervision in the feeding of an infant, maybe not. After all, nannies from the village are smarter than their age.

"All this wouldn't have happened if she stayed at home and took care of her baby like a proper woman," Melody's grandmamma announced in the living room, as neighbors and friends trooped in with food and pity.

Melody's mother bit her inner lip until she tasted blood. Her husband placed his left palm on her knee. She fought the urge to slap his hand away and slap the frown off her mother-in-law's face.

"A woman's place is at home with the children. It's no use trying to do a man's job. But Ego refused. Always work, work, work."

Ego bit her lip harder, her husband rubbed her knee in small circles. The urge became an unbearable itch on her knee. Instead, she dug into the back of his palm with her fingernails. She had planned to remove the artificial nails before the burial ceremony but she didn't have the zeal to leave the house, and the house was always busy with mourning visitors. Now the nails had found a new purpose. She dug into his hand until she felt a warm wetness on the pads of her fingers. She knew he didn't blame her for their daughter's death, but that wasn't the point. She blamed herself and she wanted him to blame her too. Instead, he cooked soft-boiled rice for her to eat and brought it into their bedroom in which she kept the curtains constantly down to keep the light out. He didn't complain when she remained in bed all through the week of Melody's death, her body smelling sour. And when she began to smolder with blame, he started sleeping on the couch in the sitting room. Her husband had a way of avoiding conflict as much as he could. It was this particular trait that attracted her to him, and at this moment, made her feel like slapping his hands off her knee. She wanted him to stop her from digging into his hand. She wanted him to tell his mother to shut up.

Melody's grandmamma was so old, her crumpled face turned her eyes into slits and gave her a permanent scowl. Whenever she wailed, the other mourners had to keep quiet to let her frail voice permeate the sitting room where they were gathered. It was somewhat rude to drown out her voice when it was obvious that she really wanted them to hear her dirge. Before she made her announcement, she had been singing the dirge for a straight twenty minutes. It used to be a common song used by women to inform others of their dead babies. She first heard the song from her mother, who sang the song for her stillbirth brother. Her mother also sang the song for two other consecutive stillbirths. At these times, she had heard the song long enough from other distraught neighbors and had identified with it so much that she joined her mother in pulling her hair, cupping sand from the ground, and spraying it in the air. But now, the mourners gathered with her had become so Christianized that they considered any traditional Igbo song pagan.

Melody's grandmamma thought about all of this as she sang. If the other mourners had concentrated on memorizing the song, they would all be singing it together. The dirge would have been melodious and soulful, and they would have known where to wail, hum, and pause. But she had to do all of this by herself, and it was a bit disorganized. This didn't stop her from completing the dirge. She even restarted it, hoping to goad them with her persistence. After letting her take center stage for about ten minutes, the mourners each found a way to carry on with their conversation without interrupting her. The ones who couldn't lower their voices left the sitting room and sat under the canopy constructed close to the porch. The guests were mostly church members, a handful of Ego's colleagues at work, and three of her husband's friends who, like him, were also Danfo drivers. The drivers didn't stay for long. After they returned from the church service, the men ate and discreetly gave Ego an envelope. Before leaving, they formed a circle around her and prayed loudly, asking God to bless her with twins.

Ego's boss left thirty minutes after the drivers. He had been looking at his watch since they returned from the church service. He was a very organized man who planned things ahead of time. In this case, he had decided to allot two hours to the burial ceremony. Which was a lot, considering that it was Friday and he had to go out for drinks with his friends and still make it on time to attend an all-night church service with his wife. As soon as it was five minutes from the end of the allotted time, he sat close to Ego and squeezed her shoulder. She was one of his most reliable employees and he had planned on promoting her by the fourth quarter of the year. Her current position as his personal assistant took her from one end of Lagos to the other. This new position would make her shuttle between Ogun and Lagos. He wasn't aware of her family dynamics. It was one of the things he liked about her. She was so professional, always so businesslike, she never used her family as bait. When she was done with her two months of maternity leave, she returned to work and, unlike his other female employees, she never asked for unexpected leaves or permission to leave the office to attend to her daughter. As he squeezed her shoulder, he was tempted to say he didn't want to lose her services.

"I will give you a raise if I need to," the words formed on his tongue.

Instead, he took his permission to leave and encouraged her to rest throughout her one month leave of absence. He wished she were a man.

Ego's fingers were going numb with fatigue. She rose from the chair, headed to the bedroom, and locked the door behind her. She wouldn't come out till 1 AM the next day.

About thirty minutes after her departure, when it was obvious that the grieving mother would no longer be able to attend to them, the guests left in trickles, till it remained Melody's grandmamma, whose dirge had risen a note higher after her announcement had waxed and waned, and when she became the only one in the living room, had become silent. Her son was in the kitchen clearing half-eaten food from ceramic plates and chucking the plates in warm water. She hobbled to him and asked for a cup of water. Her voice was hoarse. Her son told her to eat some Ukwa and dried fish. She hadn't eaten since morning.

"I told you not to marry her, but you refused," she started.

"Because she's from Mbaise and you have a problem with Mbaise women," he said.

"No."

"Yes Mama."

"She loves money too much. Money is not everything. It is the root of all evil."

Ejike sighed and took the cup from his mother.

"Mma, Ego is a HND holder and I couldn't even finish secondary school. Still she chose me."

As always, Ajero was the reason Ejike made a bet on the betting site again. Ajero was a chronic gambler who bet every day regardless of the outcome. On some days his game made it, on most days, his game was cut, most times by just a singular odd. Ajero didn't think he was addicted to Bet9ja, he thought he was persistent. He introduced Ejike to the betting site. It was 2014, a time when people flocked into betting shops to choose their odds. These shops bustled with students, salary earners, businessmen, wage workers, and anyone else interested in football and courageous enough to put his money where his mouth was. They made predictions, analyzed previous matches, argued, reconciled, but above all, believed in luck or faith, whichever terms you choose. It was easy money. With just 500h you could place an odd worth 10k and if your predictions were correct, if you had analyzed all the indicators, but most importantly, if God blessed your hustle, you would win.

When Ejike cashed out his first 10k, he became a believer. He began making bets worth 500h every day. In a week he was spending 3.5k, which was a lot but it was part of the hustle. After all, nothing goes for nothing.

Ajero taught Ejike to put all the proceeds from a successful bet into another bet. It wasn't greed, he was using money to make more money. There were mostly losses but there were also electrifying moments. Like the time he won that 100k bet. He couldn't believe it. He used part of the money to get a new flat-screen television and fix his cracked windscreen that was long overdue. Or the time he won 150k. Thinking about it made him check the time. He couldn't wait for it to get to 7 PM. Chelsea was playing Liverpool and if everything went as predicted, he would win 10m. The week before, he placed an odd worth 1k. All the matches were successful and he was just one game away from 10M.

It wasn't impossible. After all, he was there when Ajero won 5m. By that time, Ajero was neck-deep in debt. One time, his wife came looking for him at the car park and they broke into a quarrel. She held the tail of his shirt and insisted that he give her money for the children at home.

The scene was more embarrassing for Ejike whose kinsmen had advised that he avoid Ajero. *Stay away from the Efulefu. Save your money in Akawo. Slow and steady wins the race.*

Ejike should have listened, but after work, he couldn't help but hang out with him in the bar opposite the bet shop. Over cold bottles of beer and spicy pork, Ajero enchanted Ejike with his aura. This aura rubbed off on him, stirred up dreams, and it wasn't long before his heart burned with that same intensity that indeed anything was possible.

"How much you think this Danfo bus fit give us? 500k? 2m?" Ajero asked him one day.

Ejike perceived it was a rhetorical question, so he sipped his beer instead.

"I dey tell you Bet9ja na God's blessing to the poor masses. Shebi you hear say Tunde don make am abi? Him make 500k just with odd of 500h."

He chugged some beer and continued.

"I tell you anything is possible. Make you just believe. God promise Abraham Isaac, but even if it take am 25 years, him still get his Isaac. Just believe. All these people we dey laugh us today, tomorrow them no go laugh again. I dey tell you."

Two months later, Ajero won a bet of 5m. They were in the bar watching the game when against all odds, Dybala scored a goal and made Juventus the winner of the match against Real Madrid. As others cheered the winning team, Ajero dropped to the floor and rolled to one end of the bar and back. Ejike dropped his last bit of pork on the table and placed his hands on his head. He was washed with joy, jealousy, and regret. Ajero had encouraged him to make the bet, but he was skeptical. When the others realized what had happened, they poured beer on Ajero. It could have been a bottle of Hennessy or Moet but very soon.

Ejike followed Ajero to the company to receive his check. They wore laundered jackets and new pairs of jeans. They had fancy haircuts. That evening, after stashing the check in a box buried underneath the pumping machine in the backyard, Ajero threw a lavish party. Ejike was concerned that he was drawing unnecessary attention, but Ajero was delirious with joy. *The blessings of the Lord maketh rich and added no sorrow,* he quoted. For the first time, Ejike saw Ajero's wife's gap teeth. She was smiling broadly and serving bowls of pepper soup and rice to her guests. Her husband had promised to give her 1m to expand her business. She had already made the budget. She would move her business to the market in Ojota. It was busier and more organized into real stores made with concrete and windows, nothing like her current shop made out of wood and nylon. She had nagged her husband until he agreed that they move to a better neighborhood, somewhere in Jakande. There were better roads, better security, and better schools for the children.

When Ejike told his wife of the miracle, he was annoyed that she was more interested in arranging a meeting with Ajero to encourage him to save with her microfinance bank.

"Ego that could have been us," he said.

Ego, who was scribbling Ajero's number on a notepad, nodded absentmindedly.

He placed his hands on her lap.

"It could have been us."

Ego squeezed his hands when she saw his face. "It is okay."

"No it's not. Ajero told me that night to play that odd but I didn't listen."

"Ajero is just very lucky."

"It isn't luck, it's faith."

"Shebi, you are joking? Do you know how many people win 5m in this betting thing? Very very few. Ajero was just lucky that's all."

"Papa Adeboye prophesied and he claimed the prophecy. Two months later and he won. Ego, it's not luck, it's faith."

"Papa Adeboye preaches against gambling. Sweetheart, you don't know what you are saying. This was just a coincidence. Luck, not faith."

But Ejike had already resolved to attend the next miracle service for his own prophecy. Now, about twenty prophecies later, and about 50k in debt, Ejike was certain that today was his day. He would buy pork and two bottles of Guinness, just like the night Ajero won. He would sit at the end of the bar so that when the time for his victory came, he would roll back and forth just as Ajero did. He had his budget for the 10m in his wallet. He would clear the debt, pay off his rent, and take his wife to scout for a new house in Jakande Estate. He would give Ego 3m to open her supermarket, he would use the remaining money to buy two Danfos, and, of course, he would pay his tithe to Daddy G.O.

The match was to start at 7 PM. He would get home by 9:30 PM. Ego would be in bed by then. Ever since she quit her job, she slept early and woke up late. She was beginning to put on weight on her arms and stomach. She didn't even tell him that she had resigned from work. After her one-month leave, he expected her to resume work, and when she didn't, he asked if her boss had extended her leave. That was when she announced that she had resigned from her job.

"How? You have been in this house ever since."

"Titi helped me to submit my resignation letter and clear out my office."

He wanted to ask why but the question was stuck in his throat.

"So, what will you be doing? Workaholic like you." He laughed nervously.

"I'm a housewife now."

He swallowed. Ego's salary was double his monthly earnings. The rent was overdue by six months, but the landlord, who was the husband of Ego's fellowship sister, was very patient. Ego washed his clothes, swept, and mopped before she left the house as early as 6:30 AM. She got up by 4 AM, fixed her lunch to take to work, and made their breakfast. Now, one month later, he had grown accustomed to seeing her in a hairnet, reminding him of rent and feeding money. The day she asked for money to fix her hair and nails, he became still. He feared that she would soon ask him for money for a new set of underwear. Already he was spreading himself thin, saving up money for the rent, saving money for their food, and stashing 1k a day to make a bet.

But today would be different. The game started and he sipped his Guinness slowly.

It was a bad game from the start. The opposing team scored two goals before the end of the halftime, and although his team succeeded in equalizing with two penalties, the opposing team scored another goal during the extra time. Ejike should have left the bar, but his legs were weak and his ears were ringing. He tried eating his pork but it was difficult to chew. Instead, he drank his two bottles of beer and asked for another. By the sixth bottle, he was feeling warm and elated, the same way he felt when he was around Ajero.

Ego was exasperated because she felt compelled to open her house to the bewildered clothes seller. The woman got in and squatted in the passage between the living room and the kitchen. It was a small space, but she was used to squeezing herself into tiny spaces and squatting on her haunches to display second-hand baby clothes to her customers. She had a couple of clothes to sample to her customer, whose daughter she estimated to be two years old.

"Melody don die?" she asked again.

Ego nodded.

"Wetin kill am?" she asked, after a respectable moment of silence.

Ego's jaw clenched. Each time she was asked the cause of her daughter's death, she saw her daughter's death certificate.

Primary cause of death: Pneumonia

Secondary cause of death: Malnutrition.

The doctor's writing was scrawly, a rendering of squiggles made by a hen scratching the dirt for grubs.

At work, she was known for her stellar and meticulous writing. When the printer was faulty and the accountants needed a quick letter written, they turned to her for help. She wanted to tell the doctor how much she hated the writing and ask that someone else rewrite it. But Ejike told her to let it go.

"Melody is gone. Let her rest na," he said.

"Pneumonia," Ego replied to the clothes seller.

She clicked her tongue in response, and went on to describe the death of her child who also died of pneumonia. She was a new mother who didn't know how to care for newborns.

"As soon as cold enter my pikin chest, him just sick, come die like that."

But now she knew better.

"It's well," Ego answered.

"No worry, God go give you another pikin. Twins sef."

Ego nodded absentmindedly. What was it with people and twins? She didn't want twins. She wanted Melody, her first child after four years of marriage, her spitting image, from her short fingers to her tiny ears and wide, inquisitive eyes.

Ego sighed. She really needed her to leave. The clothes seller started a story about a woman who lost her three children in a road traffic accident. Ego remembered the story because it trended on social media last year. Three children were attempting to cross the road when a truck ran all of them over. It was reported that neighbors had to restrain the mother from slashing her wrists with a kitchen knife. The clothes seller claimed she was friends with the woman.

"She born twins just last month."

Ego wasn't convinced. What were the odds of the clothes seller knowing this woman? What were the odds of her giving birth to twins? What really was it with people and twins? She wanted to say that her Melody wasn't a lose-one-get-two-free promo, her Melody was an individual, an irreplaceable offer who she lost to malnutrition. And it wasn't because she was lacking anything, it was because she couldn't put her eyes down to see that she was starving, couldn't notice that Chikodi the nanny didn't have the patience for her daughter's fussiness, couldn't notice that her daughter was losing weight, till she began coughing and had a high fever that couldn't stay down even after giving her paracetamol.

Ego felt compelled to tell all this to the seller, but she fought the temptation to do so. She didn't want to be an anecdote for another woman's consolation. Just when she thought the seller would continue with another story, she thanked Ego for her time and left.

Ego went into the bedroom and began packing all of Melody's clothes into a suitcase. She didn't bother folding them but stuffed as many as she could into the suitcase. When she saw how much space the unfolded clothes took, she brought them out and folded them before placing them back. Last week, during the mid-week service, her spiritual leader told her to give all of Melody's things away. It wasn't a request, it was a spiritual directive, an instruction from the Lord. Mummy Tess had a way of talking loudly when she felt the spirit come upon her to make a declaration. Sometimes when the spirit's leading was too strong, she staggered, like the burden was too much to bear. Ego didn't bother kneeling this time. Instead, she remained seated on her chair and stared ahead. She didn't want to come to the service. She didn't want to leave the house at all. All she wanted was to be in her bedroom.

Ego took Melody's plastic bathtub to the bathroom and scoured it with detergent and a sponge. Next, she washed her buckets and her large washing bowl. In the kitchen, she washed the flasks used to store hot pap and hot water. She washed her feeding bottles, spoons, cups, and plates. She dried all these on the porch, spreading them out on a plastic wrapper.

She loved her job. She loved the busyness of the office, the customers' never-ending issues, and her colleagues' gossip. When her boss promoted her from a clerk to his personal assistant, she loved to sit in the back seat of his air-conditioned Venza, running errands from one point in Lagos to the other. She loved her office, loved wearing the suits and second-hand pumps she bought from Katangawa market. Was it a bad thing? This drive to work?

She married Ejike because, out of all the suitors that came, he was the only one who didn't feel threatened by her rigid schedule. When they met, she was working as a clerk in a tiny microfinance bank. He understood that she had to work from 8-5 PM every Friday. So no, she wasn't excited about going out on Friday nights, because she had to do laundry and sleep for an uninterrupted nine hours so she could go to the market on Saturday morning. And no, Saturday evening was out of the question because she had to go to choir practice. Sunday morning was for church service and Sunday evening was for home cell fellowship.

While the other suitors encouraged her to ease up because she was an unmarried woman, Ejike drove her to the market every Saturday morning on his bus and dropped her off at her place. He followed her to church, and on Sunday evenings, after they returned from the home cell fellowship, he took her to a suya joint for roasted beef and Malta Guinness. The first time he washed all her clothes, including her panties and bras, she stood by the toilet door and watched him, elbow deep in foamy water. That was when she decided that if he asked, she would say yes. He would let her fly, and do what she wanted. And she wanted a seven-year-old nanny, not someone older, because those nannies were unsuspecting seductresses and husband snatchers. And no, she couldn't slow down at work because she had a chance of rising to a managerial position one day. She had already made plans to commence part-time learning to boost her HND.

At the hospital, the nurses stripped her daughter naked and placed her into the bassinet scale. Ego looked at her daughter's sagging skin and saw it for the first time. The nurse said her daughter was wasted because she was less than 60% of her expected weight. She had marasmus and not kwashiorkor because she was lacking calories and not protein.

"If she had kwashiorkor, her feet, face and tummy will be swollen," the nurse explained.

Ego thought of the photos of hungry African children on UNICEF pamphlets and shuddered. She felt as if she had been caught in a rain that made her clothes see-through, she felt as if a wind had hiked her clothes and revealed to bystanders that she had no underwear on.

The pediatricians used her daughter to teach the clinical students. They rubbed her sparse brown hair, and pointed at her sagging butt, jutting ribs and cheekbones. They pelted her with questions.

"Was she exclusively breastfed?"

"No. I stopped at two months. I had to go to work."

"We understand."

"How many times does she eat in a day?"

"She eats about five times."

"And you are there to see that she eats?"

"No. The nanny feeds her."

"And you supervise this nanny?"

"I taught her how to feed Baby. I'm always at work. Except during weekends."

"Is the nanny patient in feeding the baby?"

Silence.

"How old is this nanny?"

"How many spoons of formula does she use per meal?"

"How many tins of formula do you use in a month?"

"Does the nanny wash her hands with soap and water before preparing the meals?"

Melody's breathing didn't slow down. The nurses put a tube into her nose and pushed in watery pap with a syringe. Her temperature kept spiking and they had to use an antibiotic that cost 13k for a vial. When she died, all Ego cared about was the scrawly handwriting on the death certificate that declared her daughter died from malnutrition.

"My daughter died of hunger?" she asked Ejike, after the nurse had plugged her daughter's ears and nose with cotton wool, and wrapped her with a batik cloth.

"I earn 70k a month and my daughter died of hunger? Like those children in East Africa?"

She held the death certificate and stared at it for answers.

She didn't cry. She had seen a mother hold her dead infant by the ankles, slap his back repeatedly, and command that he come back to life in the name of Jesus. She had seen a mother pray for her dead child for an hour, grunting and howling, until she became quiet and exhausted. She had seen how fast diseases took children, the nurses quickly attending to the bodies, and the doctors carrying on with the rest of the sick children. They let the mothers grieve as long as they wanted, or pray as loud as they wished until they wore out and stopped.

Ego packed Melody's utensils into a Ghana-Must-Go bag and placed it next to the suitcase. She packed all the toys and put them into a carton. Two years ago, she made monthly visits to an orphanage in Isolo, gifting them with food items, toiletries, and clothes. One time, she organized a birthday for her favorite child, a girl with a very large head. Her mother had abandoned her in a dumpsite, along with her medical reports and even a yellow cannulae still strapped to her daughter's wrists.

Ego dismantled the walker and placed it on the carton. Tomorrow, she would visit the orphanage and give them her dead daughter's belongings.

Ejike got home by 1 AM. He honked continuously, even when he heard the rustling at the gate. In the morning, he would apologize to the landlord for his behavior, but at the moment he felt like he was the owner of the house. Ego assisted the gateman in anchoring the gate, and as she approached her husband, she could perceive his drunkenness.

"Ejike you are lucky you didn't crash your motor and killed yourself," she said.

She called him Ejike when she was upset. For the past two months she had been ignoring him, she called him My Husband. Before that, she called him Sweetheart.

Ejike tried to reply, but his head was fuzzy and he had to battle with a sudden attack of hiccups. By the time he was done, Ego had gone into the bedroom. He followed her into the bedroom, stripped naked, and fell plonk on the bed.

Ego was shocked. The nerve of him. He wouldn't dare come into the bedroom if he were sober. She tossed and turned, and when she couldn't tolerate the smell anymore, she tapped his leg and told him to go take a shower.

"You stink."

"Nne please."

"Ejike get up and take a shower."

"What happened to My Husband?"

Silence.

"I know you blame me for Melody's death. I know you are thinking that if I was man enough to be the sole provider, I should have insisted that you stayed at home to take care of her. I know you are hearing me."

"You are drunk."

"You are angry with me."

"You need to shower."

"You need to resume your job."

"Okay."

"Okay."

# The Roots That Held Us

Our family reunions were a well-known celebration. Now, that may sound cocky, but let me tell you, they were held on Memorial Day for a reason. Anybody that found a poor excuse to miss them was shunned with sideways glances and met with the pettiness of not being invited to Auntie Kat's Thanksgiving dinner. One day during the summer, every root of my family traveled back to the old oak tree in my grandparent's yard. Generations of vehicles crammed into twenty acres of wide fields and sloping hills. Every person stepping foot from those vehicles had had at least one memory in this yard, whether they were distant cousins, in-laws, or family friends. Every single one of them had found a reason to enjoy themselves and come back—except me. I was the blackest of sheep in my family. Even Cousin BJ, who'd been locked up since I was twelve for selling narcotics, found a way to get a handcrafted card in the mail before that sacred day. But I had committed the worst of crimes in a Black family. I didn't believe in God.

That may seem overdramatic, but if anyone knew theatrics, it was the people in my family. I thought about that scene from *A Raisin in the Sun*, where Beneatha smoothly remarks, "There simply is no God," and gets a crisp slap across her face from her mother. So, I didn't dare flaunt my atheism to any specific relative, but still somehow, they knew. The pregnant pauses that came after I refused to say prayers. My absence on Sundays. Lastly, the most prominent of my decisions came at my baby brother's funeral, when I refused to bow my head in prayer or hold anyone's hand. I stood defiantly with folded arms, wrapping in all of my anger.

It could have been assumed that I was simply grieving and everyone goes through it their own way, but my avoidance of family events, especially those involving religion, somehow placed me on their heathen radar. I found myself being tagged in those outdated memes that quoted the Bible and, for some reason, always had a picture of unrelated cartoon characters. Then there were the forwarded messages reminding me that my brother was so special God told him to come home early. These answers to death came like the Tooth Fairy and Santa Claus, but I didn't need an answer for death, I needed an answer for hatred, something nobody could give me. So the texts were ignored and the posts were untagged, until slowly my family washed me off of their hands.

When my Honda Civic pulled into the yard, I understood why the sight of it split the conversation of old heads sitting on the front porch. I looked at the white t-shirt on my passenger's seat that read: *Davidson Family Reunion* in huge calligraphy. On the back, an image of my brother from his baseball days. A little boy with plump cheeks framing his gap-toothed grin, kneeling over home base. *We celebrate the memory of Jarrod Fields Jr.*

Underneath that was the reunion date. My mother mailed it to me weeks ago and it sat on my dresser until I finally let it guilt trip me into a five-hour drive to my grandfather's house. I looked at Jarrod's face on the shirt.

"You'd do it for me, I guess." I lied to myself. This was the same Jarrod that faked a stomach ache on Easter Sunday and left me to recite a full speech by myself in church. I stuttered through the whole thing, and after several *That's okay baby*s and pity applause, I sat down. I snorted at the memory and decided I couldn't stall anymore.

I turned the car off and cracked the door to be met with good ol' Georgia humidity. The heat carried in the smell of barbecued meats and fried fish as I approached the front porch. Somewhere on a speaker, Childish Gambino crooned about staying woke.

"Hey, there now. Who that is in my yard?" Uncle Harvey asked jokingly. His smile was lit with several gold teeth when he chuckled. "Come give your uncle a hug, Evie Mae," he said as I went over to greet the table. No matter how normal your name was, people from the country had a way of making it sound old-fashioned. In Atlanta I was Evelyn, but here I was Evie Mae. Uncle Harvey was sitting in a rocking chair so permanently used by him it might as well have been his. He was playing spades with Uncle Rev and a cousin named Junebug I wasn't sure I had met but of course I was related to because there's always a cousin named Junebug somewhere in your family, right?

"Your Aunt Kat in the kitchen. She'll be happy to see you. How you been holding up, baby girl?"

It had been five years since my brother passed, but people never stopped asking. It was like people expected you to wake up and say you forgot about the whole thing.

"I'm good," I said.

"You lookin' just like your mama, too. I ain't seen 'cha since you was a baby," Junebug chimed in before he started explaining who's middle child, cousin, and brother he was. This was something my family kept record of like military titles but easily faded from one ear to the next.

"Nice to meet you," I said, "I'm gonna go let them know I'm here."

"Psst..." Uncle Rev beckoned for me to get closer. "Gone head and put that shirt on to please your Aunt Kat 'cause she's in one of her moods."

"Yes, sir," I said, pulling the shirt over my head and stepping under the threshold. If I was a black sheep, this was the lion's den. The interior of my grandmother's home reminded me of another line from *A Raisin in the Sun*. In my mother's house, there is still God. Everything from white Jesus greeting me in the living room to the Black baby angels playing on the mantle reminded me of that line. And as if to solidify everything, there was my Aunt Kat bustling through the beaded curtains that led to the kitchen.

"Uh uh, we are not playing that music in here today."

"It's just Chance the Rapper, Auntie!" Cousin Izzy persisted.

"I tell you what, I'll give you one mo' chance to turn it off. Put my gospel back on!"

Lil' Izzy popped her lips, but not before turning it to Tamela Mann's *Take Me to The King*.

"Izadora, don't make me smack the letters of your name back to alphabetical order, lil girl." Aunt Kat threatened before realizing I was there.

"Evelyn, is that you? You can't speak when you come in? Tammy, you ain't tell me your daughter was coming." She threw her arms around me in one of those Auntie hugs that bridged the gap of time spent apart.

She herded me into the kitchen of aunties.

My grandmother's kitchen was outdated but familiar. The once white wallpaper had aged to a beige color that hung portraits of Martin Luther King, Barack Obama, John F. Kennedy, and every one of her grandchildren. To her, they all held the same importance. Every year there was a new addition. My aunts would follow tradition and hang a new picture.

There was Jarrod, twice, once as a newborn and again as he appeared on my shirt. Yesterday would have been his 18th birthday. One of my aunts would have replaced his gap-toothed face with that of a young man who had graduated from high school. I didn't even know what that face would look like. All of his possibilities were now would haves, and it made my chest tight.

"Evelyn, how's that little job up there in Atlanta treating you?" Aunt Kat chimed from over the stove.

I tried not to take offense. To her, everything you did before retirement was considered *little*, whether it be a *little* job, or even a *little* friend who wasn't acknowledged as a significant other until marriage, and even then I think I'd heard one of my cousins-in-law be referred to as a *little* husband before.

"It pays the bills," I responded.

"You know they just started a magazine downtown. Sister Mabel from the church knows somebody up there and I told her my niece, Evelyn, write for a paper up there in Atlanta. You should go look into it. Could bring you a little closer to home."

"Mmhm...I'll look into it." I lied.

Aunt Kat took it as a slap to the face when I left for Atlanta because to her family was everything and everything was family. In a town so small most of my family made up the church's congregation, everybody knew somebody that could get you employed. But I knew for a fact that whatever magazine my small town had didn't have space for my Black presence or opinions. Aunt Kat kept pressed curls, never stepped outside in anything but her Sunday's best, and could codeswitch with the best of them, but that didn't stop her from being an underpaid assistant, ten years overdue a promotion. At any moment a young blonde with less experience but a little more nepotism could get her pushed out of her position and Aunt Kat would just call it God's will.

"I just worry about you. You know we never had any kin that far north. I be hearin' about all that stuff they got goin' on up there."

"Can't be worse than what we got here," I reminded her.

"God left Atlanta a long time ago. Couldn't find nothing fit with the place. Ain't nothing decent up there." That was Aunt Kat's favorite rebuttal for anything she couldn't explain or defend.

"Doesn't your ex-husband and his new wife live up there?" My cousin, Martin, leaned against the door frame, eyes low and red with a lazy smirk, as he picked at a bag of potato chips. I could smell the weed from across the room.

"Like I said...ain't nothing decent. And speaking of decent, you bet *not* have none of that devil lettuce on you in my mama's house," she spat at him.

"Auntie, you want some?" he teased as he went to wrap his lanky arm around her.

"Martin, go on somewhere! You smell like a headache," she retorted. "Why don't you speak to your cousin!"

"What's good, Evie?" He greeted me with a familiar one-armed hug that fanned the scent of kush, liquor, and cologne too weak to hide any of it. "Don't forget, we gotta get ice later," he said with a wink, as he disappeared behind the beaded curtain. It was an inside joke between us and our other cousins.

"I sure hope that doesn't mean what I think it means," a warm, raspy voice said.

My mother came down the stairs like royalty. A halo of curls surrounding a glowing face that didn't look nearly as disappointed as it did amused. Her lips sprouted into a smile like mine, showing our matching gaps.

"Don't let Martin get you in trouble." Her face scrunched up as it examined mine. She carried grief under her wide eyes, in greyish circles, but she still looked like she had the sun in her. She squeezed my face in her soft hand. "I hope you didn't plan on coming and going tonight."

"No. I took a few days off," I assured her.

"Good. I made up the rooms upstairs. You can share with Letty. Just like old times." As she smoothed the creases out of my shirt, her eyes lingered for a moment on the cloth print of Jarrod's face. Once she was done fixing both of us, her eyes met mine again. "Glad you could make it. We missed you out here."

"Missed you, too," I said, with the most genuine smile I'd give all day.

"Do me a favor and make sure your daddy ain't out there burning those ribs."

"Yes, ma'am," I chuckled and headed out the back door. By the smell of it, the ribs were already a lost cause.

There stood my dad, bald head beading with sweat over his fancy grill. Uncle Tommy and cousin Luther were yelling close by. Their attention was far from the smoke rising around them. Dad had an accusing set of tongs pointed dead at Luther.

"Lebron! It's definitely Lebron," Luther incited. He flung a chicken wing bone across the yard and began to pick at another.

"What the hell? Tommy, you hear your son? You really think Lebron is the best player of your generation?"

Uncle Tommy threw his hands up in defeat and walked to his folding chair.

"Well, who y'all got? Michael? Y'all swear Michael the best." Luther retorted.

I picked up a foil-covered bowl and began removing the unlucky ribs with the extra set of tongs. Dad broke from his debate and turned to me.

"Baby girl, tell Luther who the best NBA player is—ooh shit!" He suddenly realized the smoke behind him and started fanning.

"Thank you, sweetheart," he said. "Hey, when did you get here?"

"Not too long ago." I coughed as I rubbed the smoke out of my eyes.

"How's that Honda running? You got an oil change before you came?"

"I—I...um..." I struggled.

He gave me the look of joking disappointment he had stolen from Mama over the years. "Evie, I know you didn't just drive three hundred miles with a change oil light on."

"Uh...Kobe! Kobe is the best player!" I swiftly changed the subject loud enough for Luther to chime back in.

"Now that's something we can agree on," Luther responded over Uncle Tommy's thundering laugh.

My dad dove back into the conversation which was picking up with such ferocity that Uncle Tommy was back on his feet. I moved backward through the grass and collided with kanekalon hair and soft skin.

"Letty!" I gasped in excitement. The look that met me was far from welcoming.

My cousin, one of the best friends my family ever gave me. Her grimace was more than a brief annoyance, but a standing disapproval that could have winded me.

"You okay? I haven't heard from you in months!"

"Yeah, who's fault is that?" she said coldly.

I wanted it to not hurt. I wanted my face to not react. I wanted my eyes not to sting when she said it. Yet all of those things happened. She had already brushed past me.

"What's your problem?" I said.

Her braids narrowly missed my face as she turned to respond. "You know you've got some nerve coming out here acting like everything is all good! Why are you here?"

My entire face was heated. Not just from her words, but the attention. Letty always knew how to draw a crowd. At some point, my uncle and Dad's conversation fell into a hush, and even the volume of Montell Jordan telling us how to do it came to a lull as everybody within a twenty-foot radius zoned in on her going off on me.

"I don't know what your deal is, but we can talk about this later," I answered lower than the three generations of eavesdroppers could hear.

"You're not even worth it! Go back to Atlanta, Evelyn."

I lost my next response somewhere between the confusion of being called Evelyn and the hand grabbing my shoulder.

"Let it go, Evie," Martin said.

"What...what the hell did I do?"

"Some people can't help but cause a scene everywhere they go," Martin said dismissively, as he lit a Black & Mild at the corner of his lip. He offered me one.

"No, thanks."

"That's right. I got something better. Follow me."

I turned back to see where Letty had gone, but, of course, she was far away from me.

My father had prompted the music to start playing again, and everyone was back to minding their own business or at least pretending like they were. My dad shot me the thumbs up with the expression of a question mark on his face. I nodded to confirm and turned to follow Martin.

We walked to the farthest edge of the backyard, where everything sweet grew. Our grandfather kept scuppernongs and plums in the little makeshift area. A few pear trees built a fence to hide the only eyesore in the yard: a rusty '76 Cadillac Seville that had been a pearlescent mint color in its youth, but was now sun-damaged into fading greys and rustic browns. There was a time when I was scared to crawl into the back because of all the dust and possible cobwebs, but over the years, Martin, Letty, and some older cousins had transformed it into a comfortable lounge.

The interior was lined in blankets and smelled like marijuana and various body mist fragrances probably still stuffed under the seats. Martin yanked the reluctant driver's door open and plopped down on the seat, releasing a small billow of dust. He pushed the passenger door open for me to join him.

"Between that dust and this heat, I'll just stand," I said.

Martin scowled, pulled a key from the glove compartment, and stuck it in the ignition. The car complained and Martin bargained with it.

"Betsy...this is not the time. Come on, Betsy. Do your thang, girl." he coaxed.

Betsy must have been in a forgiving mood, because after a few concerning whines and stutters, the engine miraculously came to life.

Martin offered me the passenger seat again. "Come on, it'll get cooler in a minute but that window doesn't go all the way up anymore. Letty broke the handle last summer."

"The fact that anything still works is crazy," I said as I joined him.

"Never for too long but," he shook out a small bag of weed, "always for long enough."

He spread out the pieces of his grinder, rolling paper, and the nuggets, prepping to do alchemy in his lap.

There was a time before all of this when Martin, Jarrod, Letty, and I would come out here to read Harry Potter and Percy Jackson, but Aunt Kat found out and called them books of witchcraft. She threw out Letty's copies because there was no sign of God in them. Ma let Jarrod and me keep our copies at home. The summer that followed, Letty said the books were childish and Jarrod became more fascinated with Pokemon. It would take a few more summers and a botched trip to the convenience store with a half-melted bag of ice to get the three of us back in this Cadillac doing what Martin called "alchemy."

"Like Nicholas Flamel?" Jarrod had asked Martin, confused by our laughter.

"Exactly," Martin said.

Jarrod shrugged it off to go play in the yard with the other cousins. It would be an inside joke we never got the chance to let him in on.

This was the emptiest the car had ever felt; I guessed this was how it must have felt for Monty and Letty without me during the years after Jarrod passed.

Suddenly, the insecurities of that moment in the yard with Letty crept in. Does everybody feel that way? Am I not wanted here? Before the thoughts could darken more space, Martin passed me the blunt he'd just rolled.

"How do you get them so damn neat, man?" I admired his work.

"Practice." He shrugged. "You used to be better than me."

"Yeah, I guess that's changed too. Why does Letty hate me?"

"She doesn't hate you."

"She just went off on me in front of everybody."

"She's just—pass my shit if you're just gonna sit there and look at it."

I took a deep inhale of the blunt and let it burn my throat. I passed it back, unable to take another puff.

"It's been five years, Evie. A lot has been going on with her." he continued.

"You don't think I've talked to her since then? I can't say much if she doesn't text back," I said defensively.

"You know Letty. She holds onto things. You'd have to be in her face to know what's going on."

"Well, what's going on?"

Martin took a hit and sighed out the smoke as he pulled out his phone. He tapped quickly across the screen to his browser's bookmarks, where he had saved a bunch of articles I'd written. He must have saved several different issues of the digital copies. He found the one he was looking for and skimmed it to highlight a particular paragraph.

I didn't need to follow along any further to know where he was going.

I remembered the night I wrote it, in my Atlanta apartment on the anniversary of Jarrod's death. I had just found out that Sheriff Eddie Pearson, the man responsible for killing my brother, was running for re-election. There he was in a thumbnail view, squeezed between his wife and a son that was almost my age, with one, two, three Black faces in the background to show what a nice white man he was. I remember letting my animosity carry me as, for the first time, I told my side of the story.

*Red and blue lights bounced off of the asphalt ahead of me. My legs tore through the pavement to reach the park Jarrod was playing baseball at. He was an hour late. He was never late. He would call. He would text. He would ask for a ride. There were too many police cars. Why were there so many police cars? An ambulance sped off in the distance but I didn't even process it at the time. Carter and Douglas, two of the boys from Jarrod's baseball team, were up ahead. Carter was crying into his mother's arms. She herded him into their SUV. Douglas was frozen up against the fence with tears plastered to his face. His white baseball uniform was soaked in blood.*

*"Doug! DOUG! Where's my brother?" I asked.*

*"Ma'am. Ma'am," a man called out, but it would take him grabbing my shoulder to make me realize he was talking to me.*

*"Where's Jarrod? I'm looking for Jarrod Fields! He's my brother! Where is he?" I begged.*

*"Ma'am, I need you to calm down," the officer said.*

*I didn't realize I was shouting or that the officer was shielding me from walking back.*

*"Where is he?" I yelled.*

*"The hospital. They're taking him to the hospital."*

I came out of the memory and back into the article that was glaring at me. It talked about a town full of racists and bigots with a Black population too busy cowering at the Oz in the sky to take action. I went into dramatic metaphors about how country folk had their noses pinched at the sky, so focused on God they didn't realize they were already in hell. It was angry and tactless now that I saw it in this setting. It was hard to look at, even from the very edge of the yard far away from the happy faces of my kin.

I remembered turning it in to my editor, Monique, who raised a pierced eyebrow at me after she'd read it.

"Wow. Are you sure, Evelyn?"

"What? You think it's bad?" I asked.

"It's passionate. That's what we want here. If this is your truth, I want you to speak it. I just want you to be sure first."

Martin passed the blunt back to me. I exchanged it for his phone. I took a deeper pull than the first time, hoping the smoke would fog out the thoughts.

"Thinking 'bout anything good?" Martin asked.

"I was thinking, traffic is slow enough that I can make it on I-75 before it gets too dark."

"Oh no. Not Evie running away from conflict."

"Well, what do you think I should do? Go back over there and explain to everybody that I didn't mean it like that. Tell them that I was hurt and angry? Give them some pathetic ass apology?"

"No, smart ass. I don't think you have to explain yourself to everybody. But, you could explain yourself to one person."

"How many of y'all read this?"

"I don't know. There's Letty, your parents—Aunt Tammy and Uncle Rod. Me, of course." Martin counted the four off on his fingers.

"That's it?"

"You're lucky everything's digital. I have a hard enough time showing Aunt Kat how to use Facebook. Luther won't pick up anything that's not ESPN-related."

I laughed. Mostly at the idea of Aunt Kat with her reading glasses perched on her nose, tapping on her smartphone as if she was waiting for the piece of technology to give her an answer. She would still have had an LG Chocolate if it wasn't for her need to show off. Luther probably didn't even know the name of the online magazine I wrote for. Like any family, they were happy to say they knew somebody doing something prominent that they could brag about in passing.

But Letty? Letty would make time. Letty would share all of my articles when I first moved to Atlanta. She would listen with delight to all my crazy stories about when I first moved there. She would keep scrapbooks with all of the illustrations she drew when we were kids to match the stories I wrote in our bedroom in our grandparent's house while we waited for our parents to get off of work. Letty would always give me time. But I guess time ran out months ago when this article was published, and I couldn't even be mad. At one point, we shared the same world. When Jarrod died, I created my own, and at some point I forgot Letty's still existed.

"You know if I go talk to her now, she's gonna blow me up," I said.

"You can sit here as long as you need. But you only get one blunt." He plucked his back from me.

"Is this how you've been dealing with this family?" I joked.

"It's the only way to deal with this family."

"Damn. Things were better when you were the black sheep. Remember when you told Aunt Sandra you were quitting high school to be a rapper?" I teased.

"Wow. We gotta bring that up?"

"What was your name, again?" I laughed, trying to snatch the blunt back.

"Nah. Just for that, you cut off, cuz!"

"Oh! It was Martini D!"

"I got my ass beat for that," he said, shaking his head.

"It was effective. Your ass was back in school the next day."

"Shut up." Martin pulled a drawstring bag from underneath the seat. It smelled like twelfth grade. In it, a bunch of body mists and overly fragrant hand lotions, as expected. I pulled out the cucumber melon mist—a favorite of Letty and mine—and spritzed some on after stepping out of the car.

"Those were the times," I said, throwing the bag back to him.

"Keep talking and I'm gonna go back over there and show everybody this article," he threatened.

"Fine. I'll just change the subject by letting everyone know you're gay," I bluffed.

"Pull me out of the closet and I'll drag you out with me, Evie!"

We joked and teased our way back into the heart of the celebration. Our uncles were still arguing with Luther. It was now one against three, but it seemed the conversation had changed from basketball to football. Uncle Rev had taken my father's place on the grill, saving all of us from having to pick char off of our chicken and ribs later. Izadora and Martin's younger brother, Marcus, had gotten fenced in by some of the aunties, coaxing them to do some little dance. The kids were reluctant and perplexed about how they were supposed to do a dance to match the beat of Luther Vandross' "Never Too Much." My mother was on the back porch fixing another little cousin's plait that had come undone. The sun was close to setting, bringing out different shades of bronze and gold under our bright white reunion shirts. I couldn't help but think...if our ancestors could dream, it would look like this.

My mother caught my gaze and inclined her head toward the old oak tree. My grandfather was planted at its broad roots, arms folded, staring up like he was waiting for answers. I strolled over, happy to escape the beautiful mural of my family. As picturesque as they were, I didn't know my place with them. So I stood beside the thoughtful, tall man and his oak tree.

"It's gonna talk back one day. Then whatcha gonna do?" I teased.

His broad shoulders shook with laughter.

My grandfather was a large man, though age was trying to slender him. He was a tree himself in both height and wisdom, with specks of silver immortalizing his curly brown hair.

"Evie Mae! Whatchu up to, no good?" he said with his usual greeting.

I was conscious that I had just smoked a blunt in his yard. So yeah, I had been up to no good.

"What you gotta say to this tree that you ain't said in sixty years?" I joked.

His smile pulled at every line on his face.

"Goodbye," he said.

I stared at him to make sure he wasn't joking.

"What? No! This is Grandmama's tree. This is her tree! She planted it when y'all moved here. She put the laundry out on it. She sat under it and watched us play in the yard. She..." I had more to say, but that lump was in my throat. The one you get in dreams that stops you from saying what you need to say. Hot tears were overflowing. My grandfather patted my back.

"I know, Evie. I know."

I knew it wasn't a decision he wanted to make, just one he had more time than I had to come to terms with. I pushed my palms into my eyes, shutting off an emotional pipe. I hated crying.

"Last summer, something told me I needed to come out here and do something with these branches. You know your Grandma hated to let these limbs get too long. They started brushing up against the back porch and that would have worried her. It slipped my mind, and you know that ol' hurricane came through here last May. A branch came straight through the window. I say, Lord that ain't nothing but Essie Mae trying to tell me something. You remember, ol' Douglas Cooper? His daddy n'em came out and helped me trim it. So I figure that's the end of it. I said all right, Estelle, you got what you wanted."

He'd been preaching for over twenty years and he never lost the ability to make any story lively.

"So then August comes 'round. I'm watching my ball game in the den. Reckon Essie mad again cause it's thundering and lightning out. You know she didn't play 'bout bad weather," he reminded.

"'Stop everything and sit still while God is working,'" I quoted.

"Mmhmm, that's your grandma," he said proudly, with a thick laugh. "Well that lightning hit so sharp, it took the night with it for a second. I heard something crack. Came out the next morning to see this," he pointed to the large split down the trunk; a crude strike leaving splinters and exposed wood straight through the core.

I squatted down to assess the damage, my head in my hands.

It was like hearing Grandma's cancer diagnosis again. It was like seeing Jarrod's ambulance pull away as I got there. I was on the ground before I knew it. One of the thick roots met me inches before I could meet the dirt. So, I just sat there.

"I just don't know if I can lose anything else," I whispered.

"We on borrowed time with everything He gives us," he preached.

I was glad my face was still in my hands because it was twisted in distaste. They just weren't the words I needed. I was indignant. I was also selfish. Selfish to have just dropped in on the middle of life happening and expecting it to have all stayed the same.

A better phrase, one of logic came to mind. *Every action has an equal and opposite reaction.* I didn't get to create a new world for myself without somehow tampering with the old one. Without the new world, Letty and I would have still been close. Martin would have someone he could be himself with. There may have been a new baby oak planted somewhere, to ease the pain of seeing the old oak tree go.

"Well, your turn. Talk to it. Tell it what you need to. May be nicer to you than it's been to me these days. And Evie," he paused as I looked up at him, "we missed you. We love you. And we're glad you came back."

He put his arms on either side of my shoulders and shook me gently with each statement. I beamed up at him and tried to let the meaning of his words relax me.

"Missed you too, Granddaddy."

He left to help Uncle Tommy set up for the fish fry.

I don't know how long I sat there. Marijuana does a funny thing with time where it lets you settle in it while it still carries on. No one bothered me for a while. The cicadas were starting to sing and the sky had played out all of its daytime colors.

"Whatcha doin'?" a small voice asked.

The cousin that had let my mom plait her hair was staring at me. She was about six years old. The humidity was already raising the poofy plaits off her shoulders again.

"I'm just thinking," I said.

"About what?"

"I'm thinking...why do mamas always put these big bows at the end of our hair?" I pinched a plastic clip that was trying hard to weigh her thick hair down.

"They keep falling off when I go play, and Aunt Kat says it's cause I need to go sit down somewhere," she vented as if this had been on her chest all day and she was waiting on someone to ask her about it.

"Mmm! See? Now why would they give you big bows on a day they knew you wanted to go play? Don't make no sense." I shook my head sympathetically.

"And it's not my fault they fall off!"

"You're right. It's not your fault. What's your name?"

"Kiva. K-I-V-A," she said proudly.

"That's a pretty name." I smiled.

She didn't know what to do with this information, so she shrugged.

"I gotta go." She jogged past me. "Oh, I forgot! Your mama wants you. She in the house," Kiva announced, proud to have remembered her task. Then she was off again, her light-up sneakers skipping over the tree's roots.

Food was very close to being ready. The house smelled like mac and cheese, baked beans, and Aunt Kat's potato salad. My mother was sitting with her back to me. Her chair pulled up to the stove in classic Grandma fashion. My grandmother sat while she cooked, and no one ever questioned her.

As if she heard me come in, my mother pulled her purse onto her lap and started flipping through bills.

"Let's see, we need...more napkins, some more of those little Hugs juices for the kids, ice and hot dog buns," she thought aloud.

"Okay," I mentally repeated everything back to myself.

"Get you and your cousins something too." She handed me more than enough.

I tucked it into my pocket and pulled out my keys.

I headed out the front door, and there was Letty on the porch in the rocking chair, flipping absentmindedly through her phone.

I sighed, heavy enough to let her know I was there.

"I'm going to the store, you want something?" After hearing myself, I immediately regretted it, but I wasn't in a headspace to talk to Letty about anything serious yet.

She continued to scroll through her timeline like I wasn't there.

"Cajun chips, a hot pickle, and strawberry soda. Got it," I responded back to her silence. Her favorite convenience store snacks since we were kids probably hadn't changed. I didn't stick around for an objection, or more stonewalling, to find out. I was back in my Honda that had barely cooled down from its sunbathing. I pulled out of the yard and headed east.

It's funny how muscle memory works. One moment I was hoping I didn't get lost on the way to the Quik Zip, the next, my reflexes were turning and stopping like it knew where to go. I didn't miss a single turn. I even remembered to drive around the pothole at the light before I got there.

I pulled up to the Quik Zip. A pile of drunk white men were standing appropriately in front of the *No Loitering* sign. One of them had the tailgate down on their obnoxious pick-ups with the big hips (that's what Martin calls them) that always have their brights on. In a town this small, when there are no bars or clubs; sometimes people just parked outside of the source of the alcohol and made it their own party.

I ignored them and made a beeline to my destination. The bell on the door rang as I pushed it, a sweet, small chime reminding me I was someplace familiar. The smell of cigarettes and hot dogs was not far behind. Not a single aisle had changed. Ms. Sharon still worked there. She was behind the counter unsticking a new roll of receipt paper.

"Hey, darling!" she waved through the new glass shield over the counter.

I waved back. I made my way through the aisles, verbally reciting my mental grocery list. Before I got to the counter, I made sure I had Letty's drink, chips, and hot pickle. I grabbed a pack of sour gummies and cheese puffs for Martin.

"Now, Sugar, you know I can't ring this up for you," Miss Sharon said to the boy in front of me. There was a four-pack of beer between them. He pushed whatever fake ID he was reaching for back into his wallet. His profile looked vaguely familiar.

"Just the jerky, then?" Ms. Sharon confirmed as she tapped it into the register.

"Yes, ma'am," said the Black boy. His voice was deeper than my memory recalled.

"Douglas? Doug?" I asked.

He turned around. A full head taller than me now, with a patch of twists on his head.

"Evie, that you?" He smiled, "I haven't seen you since..." he trailed off.

He hadn't seen me since my brother's funeral. One of the last memories I had of Doug was him in a baseball uniform covered in my brother's blood. Neither was something to bring up in a casual greeting.

"Boy, aren't you like barely eighteen? No, Miss Sharon, he won't be needing those. I'll take them though," I said, putting my items on the counter with the beer.

I gave Doug a wink to keep him on standby. He sheepishly moved out of the way.

"Hey Evie, how have you been, girly? Atlanta treating you well?" Ms. Sharon asked as she bagged my items.

"Yes ma'am, just came through to see the family." I pulled out my ID. When I reached up to slide it through the window, I noticed the large *Pearson for Sheriff* sticker stuck to the partition.

Ms. Sharon noted my hesitation and our eyes met.

"Oh, hun, I know how old you are," she said nervously. "Tell your mama n'em I said hi."

"Uh-huh," I said, grabbing my change and leaving swiftly. In my anger, I almost forgot Doug was on my heels.

"Oh! Here." I handed him his four-pack.

"'Preciate it."

"Yeah, don't mention it. You know you gotta get a good fifty miles from here if you wanna fool anybody with a fake ID."

"True. Probably about to toss it anyways. Won't need it where I'm going."

"Where is that?"

"The army."

"For real? You enrolled?"

"Start training later this month," he said proudly.

"You sure you're ready for that?"

"Can't be worse than anything here." He shrugged.

It wasn't meant to sting me, but it did. This town had prepared him, with his first dead body. I closed my eyes, waiting for the sting to go away.

"Crap! I'm sorry, Evie. I ain't mean to...," he said, registering my face.

"It's fine. I...My family is uh...having a cookout. It's over at my granddaddy's. He told me you helped him with the tree last summer. You should stop by and get you a plate."

I had my smile fixed back in place. I hoped it looked sincere.

"Yes ma'am. I'd like that."

He headed down the street toward his house. I headed back to my car. The white boys were still tailgating and were now more comfortable, with two of them sitting on the ice cooler. I stepped over a few empty beer cans to get back to my car.

Ms. Sharon didn't seem the least bit concerned about what was going on outside her store. Let these have been Black men and she probably would have hit the panic button. Out of all racism, sugar-coated, dirt road racism is the worst. It will drawl pleasantries out at you and ask how your family is doing, the whole while knowing it's only allowing you to exist until your existence threatens its comfort.

A beer can hit my window.

The men surrounding it howled with laughter. My window tint had me completely exposed to them. I glared out at their sweaty, red faces. I noted Sherriff Eddie Pearson's son standing in the back.

I stuck my key in the ignition. The engine stalled. I turned it again. It stalled. I tried again. The key gave the car life for about five seconds before it groaned at me. The angry change oil light flashed its final "told you so" before it died.

I called my dad. It went to voicemail. I called my mom, she answered on the second ring.

"You on your way, baby?"

"Mama, I'm at the Quik Zip. My car won't move."

"What do you mean it won't move?"

"I don't know. It won't..." I turned the key again to let her hear the engine herself.

"Uh uh, baby. It sounds like her engine."

"Is that Dad? Is he there?"

"Her engine failed. Yeah, I'm with him now. You drove here without an oil change?"

"Yes." I sighed shamefully.

"You chose an expensive lesson to learn the hard way, little girl."

"Can someone come get me?"

Another can hit my windshield.

"Yeah. Your dad can't see on the road at night. I'll send Martin."

"Hey, brown sugar, you need some help?" yelled one of the inebriated.

"Okay. Quick?" I asked.

"Evelyn? What's wrong?"

"Uh...Sheriff Pearson's son is here."

She promised that Martin was on the way. I don't know if the last part of what I said made any sense to her. I couldn't bring myself to say, "Mom, the sheriff's son is here and he and his friends are throwing things at my car." I clicked the lock button for the doors again and rested my head against the steering wheel.

In my new world, this kind of thing didn't fly. I'd have pulled out my phone and started live streaming. I'd have said something. In my new world, my anger wasn't penalized by my Blackness. But I was no longer in my new world, and I was just a guest now in my old one. My hosts wanted me compliant and shepherded at all times.

I heard Martin's Charger pull up before I saw it. The bass from Kendrick Lamar's "DNA" vibrated the parking lot. I was lost in my meditation until Martin's tap on my window startled me out of it. I opened my door and he took in the small space like a shield, with his arms perched on the hood.

"You good?" he asked, but his focus was already on my aggressors.

"Yeah." I exhaled.

"Letty, grab the oil out the back. I wanna try something."

To my surprise, Letty came out of the passenger side of Martin's car, just as nonchalant as she'd looked before. A whistle came from the rowdy men as Letty came over with a jug of oil. She shot a look of disgust back at them. Martin tapped the hood for me to pop it open. I flicked the switch.

"Go get in the car," he told Letty, as he inspected the engine. "I don't need you hovering."

"Then why the hell did you ask me to come?" Letty shot back.

"Girl, go get in the car," he said, breaking down each syllable for emphasis. Letty shuffled back to the Charger. Martin locked the doors before she could reach them. She snapped her head back at him, though he paid her no mind.

She swiftly opened my back door and bopped down with an aggravated sigh. I held out the bag of chips. She snatched it.

"You gotta draw trouble every damn where you go?"

"Now did I say shit to you? And don't be snatching nothing from me!"

"Why are we out here right now? Because of you!"

"What the hell is your problem, Leticia! I did not ask you to come!"

"It doesn't matter cause I'm here now. Once again, helping Evie with *Evie's* problems! Ungrateful ass!"

"What do you want from me? I'm sorry, Letty! I'm sorry that the article hurt your feelings. It wasn't meant to offend you!"

"Well, how the hell else was I s'posed to take it?"

Though the windshield was blocked by the arched car hood, it didn't take the focus of the men away from our parking lot scene. Another one howled.

"Whew, ladies don't fight," the catcaller said.

"Speak for yourself, I like mine a little ratchet," said the one throwing cans.

"SHUT THE FUCK UP!" Martin roared back and slammed the hood of the car. It was enough bravado to shut everyone up. We were all on alert. Even Ms. Sharon peeped out her side window to see what was going on.

Drunk white men? No problem. Customer with car trouble? Personal problem. A Black man yelling? Danger.

Eddie Pearson's son, who had been at the back of the crowd, suddenly rose to let Catcaller and Beer Can flank him. Letty and I stood beside Martin.

"We got a problem, man?" he asked. Somewhere between the liquid courage and his friend's reactions, he had found the audacity to look in charge of something.

"Nah, but your friends not gonna talk to my cousins like that."

"Well, why don't y'all just get out of here then," said Catcaller.

"Come on, girls," Martin walked away, but before he could take his first step, Beer Can shoved him.

"STOP!" came a ragged scream. It ripped through my throat before I even recognized it as my own. One hand gripped the bag of ice, and the other jabbed at Beer Can's chest. Letty had my arm in one hard tug to restrain me. Martin had me by the waist. It wasn't enough. What was enough was Catcaller nudging the Sheriff's son and jerking his head toward me.

"Ain't that that girl whose brother...? The one your dad..." He let his index and middle finger release an imaginary bullet. That's what my brother was to them. Not a name. Not a body. Not a human. A gesture. A rumor. An incident.

Martin let my feet touch the ground. I don't know if his arm finally gave or if he meant to let go. His jaw set, tense, though he was unraveled. Letty's eyes were closed as if she were praying. Her manicure still wrapped tightly around my forearm, but her hand was shaky. And at that moment, I decided everything that I was going to do next was worth it.

I twisted out of Letty's grip and was too fast for either of my cousins to restrain me. I raised that bag of ice over my shoulder and struck the closest white flesh I could see.

*Hi, I'm Letty and this is my security wallet. See, it's got my ID in it. I sleep with it every night. I can't sleep if it's not there. It tells you I'm a nurse. It tells you where I live. See, Breonna Taylor died and it got me thinking, she's a Black woman, I'm a Black woman. She's 26. I'm 26. I couldn't sleep for a long while, thinking what if that was me? So I sleep with my wallet in the bed so I can always be prepared to explain my reason for existing in any space, even the one that I own. This is my security wallet. My mom has a security bible. Cousin Evie has a security notebook. Our cousin, Jarrod...he has...he had a security glove. But this...This is my security wallet.*

*So, we're on the sidewalk. It's after practice. I say, "Jarrod, when you play outfield you can't let nothing sneak up on you like that. You gotta be ready at all times." He says, "Doug, I got this, bruh. You just worry about Coach letting you off the bench this season." He gets one home run out of last season and suddenly he's talking all the smack. So I say, "Show me!" I throw the ball and he's gone. I mean he takes off! I can't see him or the ball but I know he caught it and I know I'm about to hear his mouth any second. But I don't. I hear a gunshot.*

"One day, Tammy! One day and she's causing chaos!"

"Kat, you better watch what you say next," my mom warned.

"We have tried with her. We have prayed for her. There ain't nothing left but to wash your hands with her!"

"That is my daughter you're talking about! They provoked her!"

"Five years, Tammy! Them folks ain't bothered us none! I'm s'posed to believe that boy and his friends start messing with her out of nowhere?"

"Mama, I was there. They pushed Martin! They started it!"

"Martin is a grown man! He don't need no woman defending him. He should have listened and got y'all out of there!"

"Do you hear yourself, Kathryn?"

"Soon as she wakes up, I want her out! She'll have the whole town talking again. I won't have it!"

"You ain't got no say in where she stays at! As long as our daddy, Horace Davidson, is alive and well, all of his children have a home here! If he didn't kick you out at sixteen when you got pregnant—"

"How dare you!" Aunt Kat shouted.

That was it. A door slammed downstairs, blocking off any further insults. I was pretending to be asleep ever since I could hear the birds chirping and the sun put an amber glow inside my eyelids. My head was throbbing. I hoped if I laid there still enough maybe I'd dissipate. Maybe I would wake up five hours away in my bed with nothing for my anxiety to chew on. I was too scared to open my eyes to find out. If I let the sunlight in, I let in reality with it. Anxiety, regret, and anger were waiting in the room for me.

I heard the door close. I tightened my eyes and held my breath, hoping I wasn't of interest to whoever it was.

"I know you're up," Letty said.

"How?"

"Cause you snore."

"No, I don't."

"You'd inhale the sheets at night if we didn't pull them off you."

"Why are you talking to me?"

"Doug and some of the family came by for breakfast to see how you were doing. You want me to leave?"

She sat in the woven chair next to Grandma's old sewing machine. Her braids were pulled around in one long plait, covering her heart. She let go of one of my old composition books that she had tucked between her arms.

"No." I felt my tear ducts fill up. There was so much built-up frustration from years of not being able to articulate exactly what bothered me about being back home. There was just never enough to prepare me for what I was walking into. Never enough healing, enough therapy, or time.

"You know, for years I was jealous of you and Jarrod," Letty admitted.

"Why?"

"Well, you all got to go places I couldn't. I didn't go to Universal Studios. My mama would throw a fit if I asked to go camping. Y'all got to go to Harry Potter movies while I sat in Bible study. It was always church and church and more church. Then we lost Jarrod and I thought I lost you too. Mama thought that if I saw that you had stopped coming to church that I would ask to stop coming too. I didn't care about that, Evie. I cared that you weren't around."

"Sounded a little different yesterday," I mumbled.

"For the past five years while you've been off living, I've been watching this family try to survive, and they taught me how to survive too."

"Surviving wasn't enough for me."

"I know it wasn't. I don't blame you. But the problem with this family has always been we say much more behind each other's backs than we do to our face. When you wrote that article, I thought you were shading all of us. Myself included. You never told me why you hated it here. I just assumed it was because of Jarrod before that."

"It was, but it wasn't. It was more than that. Y'all just stopped talking about it!" The stinging was back. I let it in this time. " How many prayers can I sit through in church when most of the family can't even say his name anymore! And nobody fought for him! And we got so quiet and so docile and so forgiving that we let this town forget too! We let them think it was okay!"

"I know it's not okay." Letty's eyes were wet, and she was struggling.

"I don't know how to be quiet anymore, Letty," I sniffed. "But I don't wanna be ostracized either. I know you all probably think less of me because of it but I can't be here. I don't know how to be here." I was losing to my emotions and had reached the point of hiccups.

Letty got up to sit on the bottom bunk beside me. She wrapped her arms around me.

"I have always admired you," she said. "We all went through the same thing, but we went through it differently. Nobody gets to tell you how you should go through it. Not in front of me they don't."

"But Aunt Kat..."

"My mama will get the hell over it, or she can go worry God about it. But I think he might have her on Do Not Disturb."

We laughed.

"I didn't mean to get y'all in trouble." I wiped away one of her rogue tears.

"Get *who* in trouble? You don't remember much, do you?"

I shook my head.

"Well, when you were pounding that scrawny ass smart mouth with that bag of ice, his friend tried to grab you. Martin threw him. Eddie's son tried to hit Martin, I wasn't having that."

I noticed the scrapes and bruises across her knuckles, for the first time identifying the throbbing of my head with the knot on my temple.

"Shouldn't we be in jail?"

"No. Cause they didn't wanna press charges. It would look bad on his father's election. They were all drunk. The one that was throwing the beer at your car was underaged. It'll make them look like trash."

I smirked. The bedroom door opened.

"You heifers good in here?" Martin teased. He threw himself on top of both of us before we could respond. A blunt already to his lips. He struggled to light it from his awkward position.

"Boy, get off of me!" Letty shrieked.

"Don't do that here! Aunt Kat is already about to blow a fuse!" I fussed.

"Girl, ain't nobody studyin' Kathryn. I got enough for her too. Her stiff ass needs some of this." He exhaled a cloud and waved a finger at us. "I wasn't invited to *this* reunion? Seems fitting considering I brought it together."

"Brought what together?" Letty and I said in unison.

"Oh, that's cute." He took another puff.

"What did you do?" Letty scoffed.

"I invited you to come 'get ice' with me. You fell for it. I got you both in the same car talking while I 'worked' on the car."

"What do you mean *worked on* the car?"

"Girl, who the hell I look like, Luther? I don't know nothing about no damn cars!"

I snatched the blunt from his hand so it wouldn't fall.

"Letty, I'm on thin ice as it is. Get him for me."

Letty popped Martin with the pillow. He dramatically slid to the floor. I put the blunt out and flicked it back at him.

The door opened again. This time, my mother with eyes strained from crying. A headwrap hugging her curls as they rebelled over the top like a crown.

"Martin, get your butt up!" She picked the blunt off of his chest and pocketed it on her housecoat.

"Auntie!"

"Uh uh, it's confiscated. And I know where the rest is, too," she warned. "Let me have a moment with Evie, y'all."

Letty got up and let my mom slide in on the bottom bunk. She and Martin closed the door behind them.

It was silent for a while. She put her arms around me and pulled me in tighter than I expected.

"I'm sorry I disappointed you," I started.

"You tried to tell me something was wrong on the phone. Didn't you?"

"Yes."

"You didn't disappoint me, baby."

"I could have walked away."

"Could you? Tell me honestly, could you have walked away and been okay with yourself?"

I shrugged.

"The answer is no. You acted out of love. You were protecting your family. You were standing up for your brother and cousins. I won't ever be disappointed in you for acting on those values."

"You know, when we lost Jarrod, I thought that changed this family, and it did, but you changed this family too. I know you haven't been around much to see it. Letty speaks at City Council meetings. Luther wants to organize a march right now. Your Granddaddy and father are doing everything to keep that man out of another term. Were you re-cording by any chance?"

"No. I wasn't..." My words failed me because they weren't my words, but my anxiety's. It had a way of putting timid thoughts in my head, but later its validity turns to smoke in front of logic.

"You don't have to explain yourself to me. My point is we've been standing, but we haven't been standing together. We haven't been sup-porting each other enough, especially not you."

"I'm sorry I left like I did. I pushed you all out. I stopped coming to church. Prayer just didn't work for me like it seemed to work for y'all."

"Oh, baby," she pressed a running tear into my cheek, "my prayers worked for you. I don't want you to follow anything that doesn't make sense to you. Religion is supposed to bring you comfort. Family is sup-posed to bring you comfort."

"This has been too much of a Hallmark morning. Could you please yell at me about something? This is starting to feel like *Good Times*."

"Well there's the car but I figured that can wait."

"Oh yeah, the car..."

"Your Uncle Tommy is having the parts called in. Luther thinks he can fix it. But we can get you back to Atlanta whenever you're ready."

I looked out the window facing the front yard at the terminally ill oak tree. It leaned toward the right more since its encounter with Death. I thought about how we'd skip around it, tripping over its roots. All the times we counted on it for hide-and-seek and it protected us in tag.

"I think I'll stay a little while," I said. "If that's okay."

"It's okay with everybody that matters. I've got some breakfast downstairs. It's some folks ready to see you but take your time." She patted my leg and got up.

I went to the bathroom first to examine my face. A little swelling on my head and some scrapes. I used wet hands to fluff out the part of my hair flattened by the pillow. In the night's commotion there had been no time to twist or wrap it. Thankfully, some curls still held their shape.

I looked in the mirror and, for the first time, I saw Jarrod. Not in the way my therapist told me was normal after trauma, but in my facial features, he was there. My eyes widened with the same look he would get when he was in trouble. My brows etched in wonderment. He was always there.

I went into the living room, which was now saturated with the smell of bacon grease and Mom's extra cheesy eggs. Twelve eyes were there to take me in. Uncle Harvey stood immediately to give me his seat. Aunt Sandra began asking me for more details, to make sure Martin and Letty hadn't stretched out the truth. Uncle Rev couldn't stop shaking his head and praying silently as I recounted the details. Letty sat by my leg, resting her braids against my knee. Martin sat in Granddaddy's armchair, rocking with anxiety.

It was quiet for a while after I finished talking. The TV had been muted when I came in the room, but *The Price Is Right* didn't need volume to be enjoyed. I let myself zone in on the game of Plinko until someone figured they had something else to ask me. My mouth was dry and I couldn't figure anything else that I needed to say when Luther walked in with Granddaddy.

"Evie, you up!" Luther called with a quick hug, studying the swelling of my head. His face tightened.

"I wish y'all would have called me. I would have smoked they asses."

"Watch your mouth, boy," Aunt Sandra warned.

"Sorry, Auntie. I would have, though."

"You'd have done no such thing," Granddaddy said calmly.

"We gotta do something! This ain't right!" Luther stormed into the kitchen.

"Now just calm down Malcolm X," Martin said. " Last night you wanted to march, today you ready to pull out the toolie."

"I tell you what, they are not letting him back in office after this. He may not be talking, but everybody else is. Sharon surveillance camera caught the whole thing."

"Mama, what good is that gonna do when she's one of their supporters?"

"The law is still the law. She gotta hand over those tapes!"

"Naw, Sandra, your boy right. She doesn't have to cooperate and it's likely she won't," Uncle Harvey chimed in.

"What's this world coming to? Daddy, is there anything we can do?" Aunt Sandra asked.

Granddaddy looked out the screen door thoughtfully. "Reckon we should be asking Evie Mae that."

"What do you want me to do?" I asked, perplexed at what pull my grandfather thought I had.

"I want you to do what you do best. I want you to write."

"Where?" I asked, still not sure I understood.

"I don't know how this internet thing works, but I figure y'all can get the word out here quicker than we can. Calvin McCavanaugh is sure interested in hearing more."

"Who's that?"

"He's the only other candidate running against Eddie Pearson. He hasn't been here as long as Eddie, so not a lot of people have taken to him," Letty explained.

"Either way, something like this would help."

I needed to sit down. Sweat was sticking to the back of my neck and the room didn't look stable. What I heard would make sense in any other setting, with any other group of people, but here in my grandparent's living room with so many faces of wisdom staring back at me for answers, it was dazing.

My most recent memories of home were of vacuum-sealed anger and words folded over in the back of a composition book. It took years to unpack that anger and properly store it. To be asked to explode in this world that begged me not to take up too much space was jarring.

"I can call my boss, Monique. She'd let me write a piece. We don't have much pull down here but—"

"That's great! We need that kind of pull. We need to make statements on Twitter, Facebook, and Instagram. People have already started talking..."

Letty kept rambling on like she'd been a publicist for years. There was a level of attention that I didn't love. People were still staring at me like a broken vase since Jarrod's death and now there was no hope for recovery.

There was too much to do for anyone to justify any more discussion. Aunt Sandra and Uncle Rev left, thinking they could convince Ms. Sharon to turn over her security tapes.

By the time they got to the Quik Zip, an edited version had already made the news. It showed me slinging a bag of ice at a boy they called Tyler Figgis. Martin turned it off and went to the kitchen to make his social media statement. Letty stayed with me as I worked through mine. After I clicked *share*, I turned my phone to Do Not Disturb and pushed it across the shag carpet of the living room like the time bomb it had become.

My mother and father went to talk to McCavanaugh, which left Letty, Martin, and me in the house alone. With little left to take our minds off of the chaos around us, we found ourselves in the back of the rusty sedan blowing our problems out in smoke.

"It's gone viral now," Letty announced.

"Can we not talk about it right now?" I asked.

That was the last she mentioned it.

So we talked about work and our goals. I laughed about the men Letty and Martin had dated and how they didn't know they'd dated a few of the same ones. We talked about Aunt Kat and if Letty had any more understanding left for her mother. Martin let us know his plans to move soon. Letty told us about her nursing classes. We had started reminiscing by the time the sky had turned golden on us.

Back at the house, we cleaned up everything from breakfast that morning before the family got back. Aunt Sandra and Uncle Rev pulled in first
to report that Ms. Sharon was holding tight to her story that the video
she gave to the sheriff's department was the full version. It'd shaken up
Aunt Sandra a bit when she threatened to call the police back if Uncle
Rev and her asked any more questions.

My parents came back to report that Calvin McCavanaugh wanted to
meet with me in the morning. Reality slowly faded back in, so I collected
my phone. I had twenty-four missed calls. It took a moment for my
phone to keep up with all of the notifications. As Letty had mentioned,
things had gone viral. A lot of people from in town and Atlanta wanted
to know if I was okay. Several emails from my boss encouraged me to
take as much time as I needed, and also responded to my request to
speak about the incident in my next article.

Mom and Aunt Sandra got dinner started. I think cooking helped settle Aunt Sandra's nerves. If it made her sister feel better, Mom was
happy to oblige. Granddaddy was back in his recliner for the night, pouring into the word of God after such a hectic day. King James looked
Shakespearean to me, but for him this was therapeutic. Letty disappeared upstairs and Martin was knocked out on the couch.

I found myself back outside under the old oak tree with the old composition book Letty had recovered from our room. I sat on one of the
knots at the base of the tree and rested my head against the trunk.

"I'm not sure what you want from me, but I'm trying," I said to the
tree.

The cicadas made up for their silence as they hummed through the
night air. I opened the notebook to start. The binding was bent and
loose, folded pages fell out of the back. Each, a different attempt at telling my story as it began that night outside the park when my entire life
changed. I realized that some of the pages didn't match. I turned on my
phone's light so that I could see better.

This wasn't just my story anymore. It was Letty's crumpled city
council speeches written on the back of notes from nursing class. It was
the newspaper clipping of Doug talking about the last time he saw his
best friend. There were Bible verses from my grandfather's pastor notes.
Prayers from my mother's grief counseling. A letter my grandmother
started writing to our cousin in prison that she never finished. Jarrod's
seventh grade paper about what he wanted to be when he grew up.

Letty had made sure this recipe of memories ended up together in my notebook for a reason. If I was going to tell this story, I needed to start at the beginning. This was as collective as our stories could get to that.

I unfolded the aged, college-ruled paper and pulled out my pen.

I started writing underneath my teenage scrawl and finished telling my truth.

# Life is Like A Weave

She lived for these moments, when the slide of each of his fingers against her skin was like a personal branding. When she could swear he wanted to torture her, sweetly, and she had to bite the soft inner flesh of her bottom lip to muzzle a moan. He knew just how to work those hands, burrowing them deeper, deeper...

"Is the water too hot?"

Sarauniya froze mid-squirm, eyes shooting open. TJ was looking down at her with a rumpled forehead.

"Oh no, it's fine," she said quickly. "My scalp is just a little itchy, that's all."

"Okay."

He resumed his motions, long fingers rubbing against her scalp. Eyes slit against the occasional droplet of warm water, Sarauniya mused that given just the slightest encouragement, she could have climaxed right there in the cheap plastic chair.

In a few minutes, TJ was done. He touched a towel to her ears, and then rubbed it over her hair gently, the fruity fragrance of the conditioner nauseating, but what could she do? This man with his unique fashion sense, his dark skin and dimples, kept her coming back. After he'd anchored a towel around her shoulders, Sarauniya rose and walked into the main room where hair extensions and attachments of different lengths and textures hung in shiny transparent packs, and cans, bottles, and jars of spritz, mousse, oil spray and gel at various levels of exhaustion stood companionably on garishly colored cupboards, reflected in multiple mirrors which bought the modest room some space.

There were two other women inside. One was about Sarauniya's age, maybe younger, getting her nails done by the other young man who worked with TJ. Ndifreke, if she remembered his name correctly. The other was a girl, really. She looked about twenty, with false sweeping lashes that were unnecessary. Her long legs were crossed so that her short Ankara dress rode high on her thighs, her flat sandals showcasing delicate feet with lacquered nails. She had come in while TJ was washing Sarauniya's hair, and only now did she see her clearly.

As Sarauniya sat, the girl turned her head ever so slightly and said, "Good morning, ma."

Sarauniya felt something thick and hot rush to her throat, itching to be vented. But she swallowed, murmured, "Good morning," and looked away, but through the mirror couldn't miss the lingering smirk on the girl's face. Sarauniya took a deep breath and let it seep out real slow, watching out of the corners of her eyes how the girl angled her head back when TJ spoke to her, how she touched her neck when she laughed. Sarauniya wanted to say something, draw TJ's attention back to her as his fingers moved in a blur over her head, dabbing on setting lotion and fixing rollers to her hair.

Much too soon, he wrapped pads around her ears and nudged her in the direction of the hooded dryer. Sarauniya ducked under it, then popped out with a yelp, grabbing TJ's knee.

"Oh, sorry," he said, adjusting the dial. "It's okay now," he assured, nodding at her to go back. She left the skepticism on her face while she did so, but when he asked if the temperature was okay for her, she nodded. Satisfied, TJ squeezed her hand briefly and Sarauniya relaxed, a smile curving her lips. That look in TJ's eye? That was more than concern. She was no spring chicken, but she still had her shit together. She could see the girl scowl until TJ stood behind her chair. He ran a hand over her hair and asked what she wanted done. Scowl turned to a pout as she whined that she didn't know and could TJ choose something nice for her?

Sarauniya scoffed in her belly. That one? She was still a girl. She, Sarauniya, knew exactly what she wanted. TJ. And not just his hands squeezing the ends of her hair.

***

Arinola was late. As usual. *I might as well order a drink*, Sarauniya decided, and raised a hand for a waiter. A man a few feet away looked at her in amused puzzlement, glancing away when she gave him an imperious look. It took a few moments for understanding to dawn, and she snatched her hand down. The counter was dotted with servers, none paid her any mind. Growing warm, Sarauniya shifted in her seat. That was the problem with all these 21$^{st}$ century franchises: you ordered at the counter and carried a tray back to your seat. She would have done better to prepare a meal at home but hadn't been sufficiently motivated, and a traditional restaurant would have felt too formal. Now she was bound to her seat because she'd wanted someplace trendy. She would just wait. And err...look busy on her phone.

Every time the door swung open, Sarauniya looked up, and was rewarded some ten minutes later with the tall figure of her daughter. As Arinola paused at the door and scanned the room, Sarauniya took stock of the man who'd entered behind her, a hand light on her back. He was about Arinola's height, a little too fair for Sarauniya's personal taste, dressed in a tunic and dark trousers, leather loafers. He had a closely clipped beard, was good looking in a distracted kind of way. By now, Arinola had located her with a small wave, and they were moving relentlessly in her direction. The thought that consumed Sarauniya's mind in neon letters, likely for lack of anything else was: *Did men still wear loafers these days?*

"Mom," Arinola said with a smile and Sarauniya half rose to return the hug, "you look lovely."

"Thank you," Sarauniya said, gratified that her sleek dress and makeup had not gone unnoticed. "You look better," she said in return, eyes sharpening on Arinola's outfit. Her sleeveless dress was navy blue with an African-themed print in bright colors that stopped just above her knees. Manicured toenails peeped out from gold and silver sandals.

"This is Ife." Arinola gestured to the young man beside her.

"Good afternoon, ma."

Sarauniya finally looked him full in his smiling face. She saw nothing but forthrightness there, no nervousness, which annoyed her. He was meeting his maybe mother-in-law; he'd better be unsure that he would be accepted.

"Hello, Ife." Sarauniya proffered a limp hand for him to shake. He hurried to do so, the smile on his face dimming as she didn't return the pressure of his fingers. Ehen. In her day, nothing was ever certain. Still wasn't.

She sat down, turning to Arinola again. "You're late."

Arinola grimaced. "Sorry. We had a naming ceremony to attend, which started late. We couldn't even stay until the end."

Already comfortable with the *we*, ehn? Yes, Arinola had told her that she and Ife had dated for about ten months, but that had been at her insistence. From the first month, he'd confessed to wanting 'a forever with her.' His exact words. Arinola had chortled when she related this, but Sarauniya could tell the romance of it had pleased her.

Seeing her daughter's lifted brows, Sarauniya said, "So, did you get some baby wishes sprinkled your way?"

Arinola laughed. "It's called baby dust, Mom. And, no. It was a very traditional setting." She glanced at Ife, who was looking back at his fiancée, and without a word between them, Arinola turned back and asked, "Mom, what would you like to eat?"

Sarauniya felt a shard of irritation. To tell the truth, she hadn't been prepared to love Ife, likely the prerogative of any prospective parent-in-law. But her growing animosity surprised even her. They were young, obviously in love, maybe he more than her. There were the little signs that grated—Ife's fingers on the back of Arinola's hand as he said something to her, the lack of space between mouth and ear, the swift chiding look masking sexual attraction her daughter gave him, a mute promise of later delights. And that tightness in Sarauniya's tummy? She refused to acknowledge it.

"Fried rice and chicken?" Ife suggested helpfully.

Sarauniya shook her head. "I'm eating more brown rice these days."

Arinola lifted her brows. "Did Daddy send you the memo?"

If her ex-husband was eating brown rice, Sarauniya knew it had everything to do with his new wife, Chinwe. She looked at Ife. "I'll just have some moi-moi and a salad. I'd like the dressing on the side."

Ife left to make their orders, and Sarauniya turned to her daughter. "You saw your father?"

"I do every now and then, Mom."

"With Ife, I mean."

Arinola's expression turned wary. "Yes."

"When?"

"What?"

"You heard me."

"A while ago."

"Indulge me, Arinola. When exactly?"

Arinola pressed her lips together, then with an infinitesimal shrug, "April."

Sarauniya was unprepared for the heat that balled in her throat. "*Two months ago?*"

Arinola exhaled and looked away, no doubt wishing her fiancée was there as a buffer.

"What kind of daughter is more eager to show her boyfriend to her father than her own mother?"

The question was fired from between clenched teeth, and Arinola threw a response right back.

"The kind who knows that things are more straightforward with him."

"That's unfair."

"Really? Well, since we got here, have you asked Ife anything about himself? Even if only to pretend you're halfway interested? Have you?"

"You just got here, Arinola!"

"Well, most Nigerian mothers would at least have asked, 'How are you...and how are your parents?' Right?"

Sarauniya felt a prickle of shame and looked away from the accusing look in Arinola's eyes. Truthfully, it hadn't occurred to her to ask those questions. Maybe of a child, but not of the man who wanted to marry her daughter. But, of course, his parents would soon be Arinola's in-law. Even she, Sarauniya, would be obligated to get along with them, maybe visit once in a while.

Ife was on his way back, and the opportunity to apologize was lost before Sarauniya could decide whether she wanted to or not. He set a tray before her first. The aroma of moi-moi steamed in thaumatococcus leaves was beautiful, and she said so.

Ife laughed. "It is! We should consider buying some to go," he said with a look at Arinola.

Arinola's lips moved stiffly. "Good idea." The fire leached from her eyes as she began eating her coconut rice and grilled chicken. His lunch was yam pottage and grilled fish. Somehow Sarauniya had expected they would have twinning plates.

The moi-moi was fluffy with bits of corned beef and the perfect amount of oil to pepper, but she couldn't fully enjoy it. The sound of forks on dishes provided a backdrop to her self-recriminations and emphasized the silence at the table. Arinola was apparently done trying, and Sarauniya caught Ife giving his fiancée a worried look. It occurred to Sarauniya how Arinola might have described their relationship to him: an on-again, off-again, yoyo concoction barely held together by blood? She cleared her throat surreptitiously.

"So...Ife. Arinola said you resigned your job and started your own business with a friend?"

"Oh, yes. Banking can just about kill your dreams if you let it. We were fortunate to get a loan, and added to our savings, we're hopeful."

"Oh, don't be modest," Arinola piped up. "They've begun getting orders from the high and mighty."

Ife laughed. "When you put it that way..."

Sarauniya sat back, said honestly, "That's amazing. I applaud your courage."

"Thank you, ma."

She was about to object to the 'ma', but bit her tongue and continued eating. The salad had chunks of barbecued chicken while the dressing had some honey-paprika thing going on so that she forgot she hadn't planned to eat it all. The rest of the meal wasn't as tense although Arinola hadn't thawed completely and wanted her to know it. Sarauniya managed to find out Ife's parents lived in Lagos and his mother loved gardening, so she imagined a much older woman with plastic-rimmed glasses and a floppy hat. He was the last of three children, all boys, and her uterus throbbed. She'd wanted more children, but it had never happened.

As they all walked outside afterward, Sarauniya couldn't resist a parting shot. "How's Chinwe?"

"She's fine, Mom." Arinola tilted her head. "I guess what you really want to know is how she went all out: pounded yam with ofensala, fruit salad. And she and Ife got along like a house on fire."

"Well, they're a lot closer in age," Sarauniya quipped.

Arinola sighed, then with a shake of her head, leaned forward for a reluctant hug. "Thanks for lunch." With a final indecipherable look, she headed for their car with a quick glance at Ife, who'd been a few paces behind.

For a moment he looked undecided as he walked up to Sarauniya. Then, "It was nice meeting you, ma."

She cocked a brow. "Was it?"

To her surprise, Ife laughed. "It was. Thank you." She was about to toss back a *You're welcome*, when he added, "For Arinola. She's...everything."

Sarauniya tried to smile, but even that failed her. He had walked away before she could remind him about the moi-moi he'd said they would buy to take home. Of course, another Nigerian mother might have insisted on a hug, called him back to follow her back inside, bought enough moi-moi to last them a week. But she felt frozen. More, she felt like an imposter. How much of Arinola could be attributed to her? Or was it the reverse? Maybe she, Sarauniya, was the fire that had purified and thus revealed Arinola's sterling qualities.

***

It had been barely a week since the wash and set, but Sarauniya's hair was thick and didn't respond well to relaxers. Her Swiss Gold friends always said going natural would suit her best. But she just didn't have the patience. Besides, she liked how glossy weaves transformed her face, gave her cheekbones some not-quite-Naija definition. And how would she survive without TJ in her life?

Today she wore a new favorite, a floaty dress that showed off her legs, Neroli Portofino by Tom Ford loving her pulse points and heralding her approach. She entered the shop and TJ looked up from a customer's hair and smiled.

"The Mama!" he hailed.

She knew he called her that so no one would look at him strangely, Nigerians being obsessed with addressing older people respectfully.

"TJ, how now?"

"I gentle o. You for tell me say you dey come na, I for prepare for you."

"Eh-ehn," Sarauniya played along. "You for kill goat for me, abi?"

He laughed. "Goat too small sef."

She smiled, then cocked her head as she saw the woman on whose hair he worked looking at her curiously via the mirror. She filled the seat with her flesh, but her face was beautiful and unlined. The weave draped around her head was synthetic, not one of the cheaper ones. She was maybe thirty? With a ring on her finger. Sarauniya relaxed and dismissed her. She spied a covered plate on the far end of the counter, responsible for the meaty odor in the room. She would guess rice and stew. But she had seafood okra soup and cowtail pepper soup at home. She could make garri in five minutes. She hoped he would be done soon and mused that she seemed lucky this Tuesday evening. Save for the other woman, no one was waiting. Even Ndifreke was nowhere in sight. If things went her way, the night would end very pleasantly indeed.

"Where's your other guy?" She had to be sure.

"His mother is in hospital, so he took excuse. God so kind, not many customers this evening."

Sarauniya nodded and murmured something about her good wishes for his mother's health even though it meant nothing to her. She shifted in her seat and found a chair nearby to place her purse while she started putting her plan into action.

"If not that I need to do this hair, ehn..."

TJ smiled. "What happened?"

"I have a lot of work to do and my whole body is aching me."

"Oh, sorry."

"I should have asked for home service sef," she added casually, glancing down at the phone in her hand.

"You should have said so since na, Mama. You shouldn't have worried yourself, coming here."

Sarauniya glanced up, as if distracted. "Just extra money, abi?"

TJ laughed, plugged in a blow dryer. "Just chicken change for you. I no go charge you like that."

She nodded as if considering, at the same time thinking, by the time the evening was over, he would definitely charge extra. But she didn't mind. She watched him stroke his fingers through the woman's tresses as he wielded the blow dryer and felt a heated tickle between her thighs. Hmm-hmm. Those long fingers would work her well, she just knew it.

About fifteen minutes later, TJ was done. The woman rose and adjusted her skirt, admiring her reflection while pretending not to. She handed TJ some notes and after a laughing exchange with him, added one more.

"Thank you, Aunty," he said. "Till next time."

The door swung shut behind her and TJ twisted his mouth. "Some customers sef. Even after they see the fine hair you have done, they will not want to pay the full money."

"Why? It's an agreement na."

"Na so our Naija people be o."

She stood up and walked to him, careful to still keep a few inches between them. "I be Naija person, I no dey do like dat."

TJ nodded. "That's true. You appreciate my efforts."

She loved the way he could switch from pidgin to proper English in a flash, with a corresponding clean accent. He wasn't one of those regular salon guys who didn't have anything better to do. He'd been educated well, she'd asked. She sought his gaze deliberately, keeping him rooted when he would have started prepping her.

"I don't mind paying for good service, whatever it is."

At first there was a blankness on his face, then she saw when realization dawned, followed by confusion. And she knew he would war within himself about whether she meant what she'd hinted at or if he'd only imagined it. She would let him ruminate over it for now.

She sat down, and he fingered the ends of her hair. "Have you washed it?"

"Yes, the day before yesterday."

As he returned with the weave she had requested, she yawned widely, hastily covering her mouth at the last minute.

"Mama, it seems you're really tired o."

"Honestly. How I wish you could come for that home service now so that afterward I can just sleep."

TJ glanced at his watch. "Nobody is waiting so after you, I will close. So we can go."

She twisted round to look at him. "Truly?"

"No wahala. Let me just pack my things."

"Thank you, jare."

Sarauniya ducked her head to get her bag and hide a smile. Things were shaping up nicely. With a little luck they might even forget about the hair altogether, that wouldn't be a bad thing.

As TJ put blow dryer, combs, oils and pins into a bag, a dart of foreboding gave her pause: what exactly was she getting herself into? It had been so long. He was young. Not all of her parts had the same pact with gravity that they used to. Sarauniya set her chin. She was deserving of a life, whatever shape she decided it would take. Entitled to pleasure, to another body occupying space beside her. She was a woman.

"Okay, I'm ready Mama."

Sarauniya smiled. "All right, let's go." She found it gratifying that he made no mention of the plate of food which was probably cold by now. She would make it up to him.

He began locking up, and she turned in the direction of her car, almost knocking someone down.

"Sorry," she said automatically.

By the security light TJ had switched on before they came out,

Sarauniya saw it was a girl of about three attached to the hand of her mother, a tall woman dressed in leggings and a T-shirt. She brushed by Sarauniya without acknowledging her apology and planted herself beside TJ. Sarauniya took a step back but turned curiously to watch TJ look up from padlocking the lower latch on the door. He seemed to wilt.

"So you don't know how to answer my calls, ehn, Tajudeen?"

He straightened as if in degrees, said, "I've been busy, Ina."

"Of course. So busy attending to your business, making money. What about her?" The lady shoved the little girl in front of TJ. She was the cutest little thing, and although Sarauniya could only see the side of her face, she seemed a bit reserved but stretched her hands out to TJ.

TJ scooped her up, his face softening. "How are you, sweetheart?"

The girl mumbled something into his neck and he smiled. He faced Ina who looked on, face hard. "Ina, I sent you what we agreed on na, and the month isn't over yet."

"Yes, but in this Buhari economy, everything has gone up. If you had bothered to call me back, you would know that I need to buy some things for Awesome's school, change her bag..."

"Ina, sebi you're also working?"

"You know I also have parents to support."

"Because sometimes it just seems like she's all mine and you had nothing to do with it."

"Oho, that's what you're saying now, abi? See, ehn, Taju—"

Sarauniya knew her mouth had to be hanging open. Her initial irritation at this interruption had fast turned into amazement. In the small provisions store beside them, two middle-aged women and a man looked on avidly.

"Look," TJ was saying, "this isn't the time or the place. I have a customer to attend to."

"But you're locking up na." Ina's voice was rising. "Who—?" Then she turned to look at Sarauniya, who belatedly wished she had retreated to the safety of her car. "This mama here? Oh, she's too big to sit in your shop and do her hair, abi? You're going to do home service, ehn?"

TJ kissed Awesome and set her on the floor with a few whispered words. "Ina, I'll see you later."

"Are you sure it's only hair you're going to do? Who is more important: your daughter or this woman old enough to be your mother?"

Sarauniya sputtered, the words coming fast. "Who the hell do you think you are?"

"I dey lie, you nor reach to born am?" Ina shot back, her switch to pidgin taking Sarauniya aback. The sneer on her face belonged on a TV screen. "I know una, na. Women wey don pursue their husband comot for house. Now your toto wey don slack don dey scratch you, ehn? You dey fin' who go wind am for you."

The silence that fell was a pressure on Sarauniya's ears. TJ's face was etched in shock, and the trio from the provisions store was looking at her with a new speculation, the expressions on the women's faces turning judgmental. The young people around the maisuya across the road had also turned to watch the drama. The eyes, oh Lord, the eyes. Everyone's attention was fixed on her, no doubt expecting a comeback.

Ina's eyes flashed in triumph, her mouth twisted in a cruel smile. Sarauniya began to shake. But she couldn't, wouldn't, lose her composure before this slip of a girl. Younger, even, than Arinola.

She snorted. "You nor get sense, abi? Is it not the same money he's trying to make to support your daughter that you're driving away by talking to me like that? I won't stay here and be insulted."

"Ehn, go na." Ina was unrepentant. "Go and look for your mate."

Sarauniya shook her head. "No wonder he has refused to marry you." A wild shot, but she guessed she had hit her mark when Ina's face turned livid. She spun around, deactivating the central lock on her car with a jab of her thumb. She heard quick footsteps coming behind her and for a moment dreaded it was Ina's. But as she wrenched open her door, TJ's face appeared.

"I'm so sorry, ma. Please don't be annoyed, abeg. Please. Don't mind her."

She couldn't even look him full in the face, she was so upset. "Later," she said, although she had no intention of ever coming back. He hadn't even said anything to halt Ina's words, hadn't even tried to shut her up. God.

She slammed the door on his face and peeled out. She kept a lid on her emotions as she drove home, although a stubborn tear forced its way out. She entered the estate with barely a wave for the gateman and parked in front of her flat, marvelling for a moment at the miracle of reaching home unscathed. It had begun to drizzle and she forced herself to come out and open her front door. She threw her bag in the direction of the sofa on her way to the bedroom and sank onto the bed.

The tears were a furious start-stop-start. Without finesse, without pretense, the sobs accentuating her aloneness. Her dress seemed tacky now, she might never wear it again. *Wear it?* She might never go out again. The ridiculous thought surprised her into a laugh, and then the tears started again. Behold her life.

When the tears had subsided, she took off the dress and took a warm bath, dressing in a sweatpants outfit crafted more for fashion than for actual perspiration. She stuck the seafood okra soup and cowtail pepper soup her maid, Rita, had made, in the freezer, pots and all, made herself an obscene mug of Milo and a stack of buttered toast. Only when she was curled up in her favorite stuffed chair did she retrieve her phone from her bag and call her ex-husband.

"Sara."

Sarauniya shut her eyes on his voice, feeling that familiar combination of peace and loss. "Maye."

"Are you okay?"

She chuckled. "I'd better be." And because she could share what had happened with no one, she said, "I met Ife. Finally."

"What did you think?"

She was silent. Ife was someone who she knew would grow on her. Although he tried to please, it was obviously out of a respect for her and not because he was overly anxious to be liked.

"He seems very focused," Maye said when she didn't respond. "He knows what he wants."

"Our daughter?"

"Among other things in life." He sighed. "I went by the store today. The girls told me you haven't been going there. And that you asked them to report to me?"

"Oh. Yes."

"Sarauniya, I don't—That store is *yours*, you're the one who wanted your own business, a boutique where you could 'express true fashion sense'."

"How is it you never forget that phrase?"

"You don't have a regular job anymore, so what exactly do you do with your time?"

*Get told off by girls half my age.* Sarauniya inhaled slowly, let it out. "I didn't call you so you could sermonize, Maye."

"Well, isn't that one way some people hear the truth?"

She took a sip of her now warm Milo, realizing that, whatever he said, she wouldn't trade these few moments for anything. How could she explain that forcing him to be involved with the store meant they still had some tenuous connection? That she was afraid being totally independent meant she would never have the right to share even a few minutes of his time over the phone?

"Okay, I'll try." Maybe for one week.

"Thank you."

*There is nothing else to say,* she thought. She didn't want to ask after his wife. She would not.

"Um...something you should know before you hear it from anyone else."

The hesitation in his voice gave her pause. Her heart jumped. Were he and Chinwe splitting? Was the oh-so-perfect relationship headed for the rocks?

"What?" She tried not to sound too eager, waiting with bated breath.

"Chinwe is pregnant."

Sarauniya blinked. And then again. "Wow," she said finally, deflated. "She obviously didn't ask you to tell me."

"No. I just thought you should know."

*Why? Does he think we're one large extended family now? Buddy-buddies?* She chuckled. The tears were threatening again. "Congrats," she said. "A boy?"

"Does it matter, Sara? Anyway, it's too soon to know."

"Well, extend my regards to her."

"Okay."

They both knew she didn't mean it and that he wouldn't.

"Good night."

"'Nite."

As she disconnected, she saw an SMS had come in about thirty minutes before, likely when she was still bawling. It was from TJ.

*So sorry again, ma. Sometimes we make mistakes with people. I regret my relationship with Ina, but I have a responsibility to my daughter. Please find it in your heart to let bygones be bygones. Please don't let what she said affect your patronage. I remain loyal and look forward to more opportunities to serve you well.*

Her 'patronage.' Sarauniya's lips twisted. She wanted Ina to suffer so badly she could taste the bile on her tongue, but not enough that she would voluntarily share the same space with that witch ever again. Having calmed down, she knew she wouldn't go ahead with the big chop like she'd sworn on the way home. And TJ's penitence just might work to her advantage on a rainy night. But he would grovel.

# The Secret

She wasn't on his mind. When he opened the car door hard enough to hang on, he didn't think of her. He didn't say *Lucy won't forgive me for this* as he licked his lips for salt.

The front seat was smelly and cold, but not cold enough. Glassy-eyed, Hewitt reached over the console, stuck a straw in his mouth. He sipped flat Coke. In the old days, Orleans would give him cola for breakfast instead of milk, as if that's what good mothers do.

The sun, what he could see of it, was a bent shape in a sooty sky. While Hew squinted past the windshield, Lucy never appeared in the dark space of his thoughts. That's how far he had fallen. Six months ago, he thought of Lucy like a sweet syrup. Now, nothing.

Even though he felt three years dead, last night it occurred to Hew how important intention was. To be who you say you are. While drunk on Crown Royal and nostalgic, he thought of his first car, a red Jeep he gave away once he enlisted. He tried to get it back because he felt lost without some memory of the boy he was. Hew even offered the new owner five hundred but she wouldn't take it.

Considering his size, Hew crawled exceptionally well. With his knee bent, sweatshirt dirty, belt missing, shoes scuffed, his freight eased into the back seat of the car. He held in his right hand his daddy's favorite toy, a dull glazed Glock he inherited once Big Earl made his transition. As if it needed to ripen, Hew rarely took it out the box.

The Glock at his side, something made him think of his mother and he thought of a dress Orleans always wore, red and blue stripes on the skirt, and he thought of how she didn't—wouldn't—hold Hew's hand on his first day of school, and he hated his mama for that, for knowing nothing about what he needed.

He wanted some music, and a blues song almost made him change his mind about the whole thing, Bessie Smith singing about sugar in a bowl. He became lost in the staccato. Suddenly, Lucy entered his mind, a sweet image of her pouring lemonade in her kitchen while he sat at the table and watched her ass jiggle. He ravaged her beauty with aching eyes. Every day, it seemed. Hew was sorry to do this to her and he wrote a short note, then swallowed more inhales and closed his eyes while Bessie sang about grief. One hour passed and then another. Finally, Hewitt Mark was weak enough to disappear.

The Black cemetery was one mile west, on the corner of Pickford and Duluth Road.

Apartments used to be across the road, a convenience. But the apartments were torn down after a long fight about tainted sewage. In its place, a glossy strip mall did brisk business, particularly Nail Palace and Braids by Benita.

Entering the 7-11 for a pop and then walking across the road to buy a mag at the newsstand on Croft and 5$^{th}$, Lucy was procrastinating. Eventually, she made it inside the funeral home. She watched, with a smirk, Colby Slender, who was lean in the chair. He had deep eyes, like a monster, and his skin was pallid. He said, "You know what this means don't you?"

"No. I don't." He was going to preach. She could feel it coming, something about burying a white man his own folk didn't want. How she was bringing a curse onto her kin.

"We have sides for a reason. What about the flag?"

"The way I see it, that flag is mine too. It's about my blood, right?" Lucy swallowed some orange pop and rolled her eyes away from the interior of the office. There was a large door that Colby kept open, and beyond it she could see a dark hall and a drinking fountain.

"Why, you got to be different all the time? Lucy it is *your* blood but not your flag. It's not for you."

"What you know about what's not for me?" Years ago, when he first moved here, Colby had been a strange outsider, an Ohio transplant whose mother gave up and sent him to live with his daddy. Paul Tolson was the undertaker, a big thing in this part of the world, but Colby didn't have fresh sneakers. "I don't care about your sides or flag or none of that race nonsense. He needs to be buried. Otherwise, he can't make it."

"Are you feeling all right, Red?"

"Don't call me that!" Lucy snapped. "We're not in high school." Red was her nickname because there used to be a strand at the top of her head that, when the sun hit, looked dark like wine. But time and grief had faded it back to its natural color of swampy brown. She was too old to give off illusions anymore. "I'm not asking you to do this. Did you hear a question in my voice? The man's dead as a grasshopper on Sunday. He needs to be buried. I'm paying. Leave the rest of it alone. It's really none of your friggin' business."

He swallowed the same way he hauled dirt, loudly. Lucy had cash, three crisp $100 bills. She still looked like the Lucinda who he danced with that one time in the church parish hall. That night holding her, he felt so much pleasure until she just walked away after Luther stopped singing. The insult still stung.

"What you thinking about?" she asked.

Colby kept staring. She was hiding something, and he had figured it out. His entire body hummed with the knowing.

Hewitt and Lucy, they had a thing.

Lucy was late for work and walked up the back stairs to the employee entrance. The hospital used to be a coloreds-only place a long time ago and then it became a hospital for coloreds and sick animals, and then the animals had their own place to tend to the wounds, and it settled into a warehouse for every Black person with AIDS or cancer or shot in the back by the local cops or needing tonsils pulled. It survived by mercy. Medicare and Medi-Cal subsidized it into staying open. But the trauma center was a subdued bare bones bunch of rooms with the most urgent cases transferred out to High Point.

On the third floor, Lucy hung up her coat, washed her hands in a bathroom that had peeling paint and exposed pipes, but the water was still lickety-split hot. She checked herself in the mirror. Quietly, she remembered that Hewitt was dead. She still had yet to cry about it. She sucked in her stomach and her tongue was dry. She noticed a few strands of hair were coming out her braid. She was thirty-three years old, unmarried, mother of a pre-teen who lived with her father.

Her mother died when Lucy was four. Her three brothers and two sisters were separated. Lucy went to live with an aunt and uncle outside of Atlanta who volunteered to take in Lucy and her sister Rhea but not their sister Blue. Blue went with a cousin in North Carolina and then she was thrown into foster care. Lucy lasted two years with her aunt. When Aunt Toe took a switch from a roseberry tree and welted her skin she took the bus back to Mayville to stay with her oldest brother who was in dental school. He lived with his bride, and Pammy agreed Lucy could move in the attic room.

Fourteen years after that first night in the attic and eating saltines and pickles, her life averted disaster. Lucy and Hewitt Marks went on a blind date.

Sophie Priest was a Labor and Delivery transfer, and when Lucy walked into the room, Sophie had her eyes squeezed shut like her eyes were her lips, as if she was determined not to look in the room. Lucy shook her shoulders. "Sophie open those eyes. I know you not asleep." With the blood pressure cuff wrapped around her arm and Lucy squeezing, Sophie finally came to. Lucy put the thermometer in her mouth. Greta Train, the nurse before Lucy's shift, had pulled the blinds open and the window was a pit of darkness. Here and there, a car drove down Duluth Road, but other than that it was isolated. "Your temp is down, but 101 is still high. How is the pain?"

Sophie just stared.

Sometimes Lucy hated teenagers. "Count for me, please. Pain. Is it worse than an eight?"

Sophie nodded.

"Worse than a five?"

Sophie shrugged.

"Okay, good. That's progress. Was your mama here today?"

Then she spoke. "Yes. And my Aunt Vera. And the lawyer for my daddy?"

"What did he want?"

"I'm going to have to testify, and they want me to say it was my fault, that I knew what a baby would mean for his reputation. That I somehow started everything. He called me a Jezebel."

Lucy checked her bandages. The swelling was worse on her legs, where the iron cord and belt buckle pulled her skin apart. Her daddy beat her bad, trying to kill the baby that was growing. Lucy thought of the beating Aunt Toe gave her, how she had to wrap cold towels around the wounds for a week. "You're coughing?"

Lucy read the notes.

"It's cold in here."

Covering her up with more blankets, Lucy ordered blood tests and a chest X-ray. "Tomorrow, I'm going to have Athena come up. She works downstairs in the laundry, but she also is at cosmetology school. She can fix your hair, so you look pretty. I know you feel not like yourself, but things change." Just then, she thought of Hewitt and reprimanded herself for the lie. Things rarely change. But Sophie was the daughter of a preacher. She was trained to think things Lucy just did not. "I'll be back in a little bit. It will be time for more Percocet." She turned. "You are not a Jezebel."

In the hall, she ran into Dr. Barnett, who wanted her to check in on Room 465, a patient who was near one hundred years old. Her gout had flared up. "She says no one has been in." Lucy wanted to roll her eyes. There were three nurses on this floor for eighteen rooms. "How is Sophie?" he asked.

"Fever. She ate a little dinner. I changed her dressing. They are pressuring her about testifying. Can we cut down the visitors to her room? Her mother only."

Rye Barnett leaned his head against the wall, exhausted. This was the kind of southern medicine not taught at UVA. "The baby is hanging on though. Already has a foster family from High Point."

"Wow. Lucky kid." In a way, Lucy felt sorry for Barnett. He didn't understand the chalk.

Confederate. BLM. Downtrodden. Uptown. But beauty. If you squint your eyes when the sun rises.

When she signed for Hewitt's body, she was given an envelope with his personals. The clerk in the morgue was itching to say something about Black woman Lucy being responsible for a white man whose daddy wouldn't sell spit to a Negro. She felt the clerk's eyes burning a hole in her back as she walked out the door with her secret.

If they ever found out, her brothers would be furious. There were three of them. Macon was the oldest, with buttery fine skin and curly hair. He had a pediatric dental practice on Cicery Street. Josiah was smaller; in school he was beat on because he was pretty like their mama Ilene. He worked as a landscaper and made the most money out of all the Carruths. He designed gardens for the big houses on Crabtree Road. Otto was a photographer with his own studio and did freelance work for magazines when he wasn't taking photos of wedding cakes. They looked at Lucy as something they owned, like a small pet, say a kitten you want to tuck under your arm. If they knew about Hewitt, one of them would have come running over with a lead pipe and a threat.

Driving home, she remembered the last time she saw Hewitt. He was in the diabetes clinic. In the middle of talking, Lucy sensed he was ready to make a promise. That he wouldn't pretend anymore. His brain was really hurt. Mid-sentence, Lucy was paged about Sophie, and she ran to Labor and Delivery and told Hewitt, "Don't leave," but of course he had. Now she had the envelope with his things and in her tiny kitchen she unsealed it. Car keys. There was his wallet. His driver's license picture was how she remembered him when he was happy and before PTSD ruined his soul, a lopsided grin, quiet steel gray eyes that looked stolen, one brow bigger than the other, a bulky nose for a white man, uncombed hair the color of sand. He had $50. There were a couple of debit cards, his insurance, a lotto ticket, two condoms, and a few pictures. Lucy recognized his mother. Orleans was the waitress at the Days Inn. In one picture, she had a bag of ice in her hand. It looked like they were somewhere near the Mary Creek. The junipers and eucalypti spooned each other. Orleans tried to smile for the camera, but her face was always too tight for anything to look more than fealty. Hew had another picture of her when he was a toddler. Orleans had a cigarette hanging from her lip, a red-tinged brick fireplace behind her. She was talking to someone because her mouth was trying to keep the cigarette from falling out while she said something. Lucy couldn't imagine her pain. Hewitt shot himself in the heart. Orleans was Baptist. That wouldn't sit well with her, probably why she left him in the morgue.

Behind the money, in a hidden wallet zipper, there was a folded piece of paper. Lucy opened it, read her handwriting. She had given him her phone number one day when he'd come to the house. He hadn't been home a month when she saw his car out in the drive. She ushered him to the side so her brother Macon wouldn't see. Hewitt had the letters in his hand and said he wanted to thank her.

Lucy shrugged. "No need to thank me. I was being a citizen."

"You don't know how much I needed these letters. No one wrote to me. Not even my momma. My sister didn't. But you did." He touched her hair and Lucy took a step back. "Why Lucy?"

She tried to find the answer, but she wasn't sure of anything anymore. Her daughter left to go live with her father. It had been a short and volatile marriage with the police called out several times. The last time Wyatt was hauled off to jail, Lucy had enough, told her brother about the mess and that was that. She was divorced with a nine-year-old. "I thought you might be lonely over there. I like to write letters. I didn't think it would do harm. You didn't answer me back."

"I couldn't." He looked away as if someone was behind him. Those damn voices. "I just couldn't. I don't think you understand."

"I'm a nurse. I do."

He weighed what to say next and it surprised Lucy that he asked her for her phone number.

"Why?"

"I don't know. A blind date."

Lucy felt reckless and wrote it down. "You obviously don't know what a blind date means. You don't know the person. After those letters, I feel as if I know Hewitt."

He walked away but said in the cool air, "Not really. You don't."

Lucy's oldest brother was waiting for her when she finished her shift. Macon was hanging in her door jamb with a bag of peanut butter and cereal in his hands. When she moved in with him after Aunt Toe locked her out, he tried to be the stand-in for her father, but her father had been upstate so long she hardly remembered his face. Her first full day in his house Macon had given her a written list of rules and then said he wouldn't follow her around, but that is what he ended up doing. Asking folks to watch and report to him, but once he saw her grades, he backed off. She really was studying at the library.

Lucy had wanted to be a nurse ever since her mother died; she remembered all the blood on the bathroom floor staining the tile. In her dreams, she would find herself sometimes swimming in it, from the shallow to deep end. Her hair and lips would be ruby red, but she was still brown as a clover in the hot light, so it didn't make sense.

She warned Macon, "Whatever you are going to say just don't. I have had a long night."

She shut the door and he walked in behind her. He never understood why she needed her own apartment, why she couldn't keep living with him and Pammy. She went into the kitchen and started coffee. She tried to feel something, but Hewitt's death had ruined her.

"Is this you just being nice? Do I get a cup?"

She handed him one when it was ready, sat in a dining chair. "How's Aron feeling?"

Aron, Macon's son, partied with a group of kids who hung out on Duluth and the low Fifties. She'd been called down to Emergency twice because Aron had drug accidents.

"Since when are you giving wife beaters money?"

Lucy exhaled. He wasn't here about Hewitt. He didn't know. Colby kept his trap shut. Macon was talking about the money she gave her ex. "It's so Miranda can go to cheerleading camp. Wye said he is in a tight place. His hours are cut at work, but he promised it was temporary. I had it. It's no big deal. It's for Randi anyway."

"Cheerleading?" He scoffed.

"And he's not a wife beater. Don't call him that. One day you're going to slip up and Randi is going to hear you."

He stared at her as if he wanted to tell her something, and she wondered if he knew about Hew. It had bothered Lucy when she lived with Macon all those years that he had never hugged her, never given her a kiss. She had tears aplenty, but he never wrapped her in his arms to console her. None of her brothers had, and it made her think it was endemic to men, a sort of code, that women are not to be touched when they are ill.

"Sis, he put his hands on you. That was enough for me. I just don't want you supporting him. You're giving money to Blue and you won't listen to me about how stupid that is, but at least she's family. Wyatt is a grown ass man who can handle his own mess without baby momma bailing him out." He drained the last of the coffee. "Anything else I should know about?"

There was a moment when she wanted to confess. She really wanted him to know about Hewitt, but to talk about Hewitt would mean she would have to talk about being married and lonely and writing letters to a soldier in Afghanistan. She would have to talk about their blind date and, in the middle of it, Hewitt sliding across the banquette seat and kissing her without apologizing afterward. She would have to talk about Hewitt's leg, the right one. He pulled it off when they were together in a Best Western hotel room.

The first time Lucy saw his stump, she told Hewitt to shush his sighs, she was a nurse, but she knew he ailed. His missing leg was a ghost. What was left was sorrowful, and she ran her hands around the detritus, an up and down motion while he let out moans that sealed the room in pain. Was she hurting him?

Lucy had been a volunteer with Doctors Without Borders, and when Ebola struck Nigeria she was horrified. The flesh of children turned into soppy gravy as they were dumped into graves. Running her hands around Hewitt's cut-off leg, she admired the way it sweat, and the moistness in her hands. There was something peculiarly graceful about it, even as it was one of the reasons he was dying. But Lucy couldn't tell Mason that.

She couldn't tell Mason she wouldn't make love with Hewitt in his pitiful apartment that she had to sneak in and out of because the Confederate flag hung over his bed. Mason wouldn't understand needing someone, that a girl who never had a mother is abnormal, always seeking something she can never find. She is a wanderer. A visitor in the white world. She chews fat the wrong way, reads books she will never understand, cries for white men.

"No, there is nothing you should know."

It took her four days, but she finally cried in the shower. She had just talked to Randi, and Randi's voice, its puerile detritus, always set her back. Each time they talked, Lucy wanted to crawl into the phone and grab her daughter's bones. Randi loved where her father lived, his apartment looked over a bunch of trees and a creek, and they even had a small puppy. Lucy felt like a stranger to their world, not seen and totally forgotten.

Randi talked for twenty minutes about the cheerleading camp, and Lucy bit her tongue while Randi ambled on and on. Lucy wanted Randi to care about science the way she had when she was that age, but Randi wanted to make TikTok videos and bake brownies.

"I have to go, honey." Lucy hated to cut the conversation short, but the grave was being dug at eleven and she had to be there.

In the shower, she leaned her head on the tiles and wept because Randi hung up the phone and didn't say her usual *I love you.* Lucy felt alone in the world. She planted her palms on the tile and heaved. She knew Hewitt was going to die, but she couldn't save him. He was just too far gone into his depression and Lucy had no one to call. Orleans would be suspicious if Lucy called her. Hew's sister, Mona, was this ghost-like figure that Lucy would see out and about but they didn't really speak, even though they had shared an English class at Jackson High School.

Trained in disaster relief, Lucy felt incompetent when grief was large like this. She settled on the facts, that Hew was tortured by the war and that torture he could never run from. Their interludes were just that, small pieces of fractured light that couldn't keep either one of them warm.

She didn't call it a funeral. A funeral was for family and friends, and at a Black funeral someone was supposed to wail and fall atop the coffin and nearly faint before an *Amazing Grace* serenade set the sanctuary on fire. This was quiet and sterile, a grave digging.

Lucy watched as Julius made incisions in the dirt. Julius was Colby's half-cousin, a cocoa-skinned man who was covered in sweat. His hair glistened. He worked at the packing plant when he wasn't doing odd jobs at the cemetery. It was warmer than usual, the sun was a leached yellow on her shoulders and Lucy removed her sweater and tucked it beneath her arm like laundry. As she watched Julius, she envied him, this job. Just being out and digging. No one to worry about, no lives to save. "This about it", he said. Just then another man she'd never seen before joined them. His name was Drum. He picked the casket up the same time as Julius, and together they put it in the ground. They looked at Lucy. Waiting. But she was thinking about the math and how it takes two men for the dead.

She moved forward. For some reason, she wanted to wear heels today, to look as sexy as she could. The dress was one she bought at a consignment shop, and it had long and fluttering folds; it was pink with white circles. Lucy unfolded the American flag and draped it over the coffin like a tablecloth. She and Colby compromised that the Confederate flag would be inside the casket. Lucy cocked her head to the right to keep a tear from falling. She didn't want these Black men to know she had tears for a white man. She opened her journal and read, "To God Be The Glory. Take him Lord." She looked up, uncertain. When Julius and Drum started to throw dirt into the grave, Lucy said, "Stop. Wait." She didn't want this to be the end, she didn't. She wanted to crawl in the ground with Hewitt and save his brain. Hew told her how he couldn't recognize the color purple anymore. He saw it and thought it was red. Everything was blood red. "If you can't take the thorns, you shouldn't have the rose." It sounded like she was blaming him, but it was the only thing that came to mind. Anne Bronte, 12<sup>th</sup> grade Poetry revisited at the worst moment.

Julius and Drum kept on pouring dirt.

She stood there for an hour. The sun beat against her face, drying all the liquid out, and she was too tired to move. As Lucy turned, she noticed someone near her car, someone white. She could tell by the willow tree of a figure and the dirty blonde hair. The closer she came to the road the more Lucy began to get nervous, like someone might take her to jail for burying Hewitt here, for claiming him. She noticed it was Hewitt's sister. Mona. Lucy had left a message on her machine when the five days had passed and no one had claimed Hewitt, and he was about to be taken to the poor people's grave.

"Hi," Mona said, tucking a strand of hair behind her ear, and it was the first time Lucy could remember Mona talking to her. In that class they had together, they were in the same group for an oral report on Macbeth but Mona rarely came to the meetings to prepare but got the same credit as everyone else. Hewitt had graduated by then and was in the war.

Lucy stared in the distance, held on to her purse. A lot of cars were at the hair braiding salon. *Must be a wedding coming up.*

"You shouldn't have done this, put him here. Momma will have a conniption if she knew, but she won't, right? She won't know." Mona was passively threatening her not to say anything about a white man in a Black man's cemetery.

"Your mother and I don't run in the same circles. Unless she's in the hospital."

Mona exhaled. "Is there anything of his that was left? Momma said it was my job to clean out his place, but I'm going to have David Peter do it. That's a job for a man." David Peter was her husband, a classmate Lucy barely remembered, but when he saw her around town he was agreeable. The last time Lucy saw him, he was buying a sack of fertilizer, dragging it to the car, and he stopped to stare at Lucy's cart of motor oil. Hew's family gossiped about her all the time.

Lucy handed a manila envelope to Mona. "That was all that was with him when they found him. His wallet and car keys. He didn't leave a note."

Lucy could lie with a straight face. He left Lucy a note, an inadequate apology for missing their movie nights. Lucy took the note, wishing it was more, something poetic and beautiful. Also, she took a lovely vase that Hewitt had on his nightstand. It was blown glass, a sculptural vase he was given by one of the Muslim widows over there as a thank you. When she looked into the glass, Lucy could see her reflection.

"I don't care what Momma say, I'm glad you brought him here. So many trees. He'd like that. What are you going to put on the marker? I want to know so I'll know where he is."

Lucy hadn't thought that far. "I don't know. Maybe *Peace I wanted. Peace I have.*"

Mona stared at her just as Julius came toward them.

"Ma'am," Julius said to Mona barely in a whisper like he was scared of her. He handed Lucy a plastic bag with some of the burial dirt, his head bent. It felt strange, and a mockery in her hands, and Lucy wanted to be rid of it. She handed it to Mona, grateful she was there to take what she never wanted in the first place.

"Here."

"What I want that for?" Mona dropped it to the ground. "You've always been a strange bird Lucy Carruth. But my brother loved you."

Long after, Lucy thought about Mona's last words, that Hew loved her. But it was in secret, so it wasn't wide or symmetrical enough. It was a dutiful sort of love. As Lucy drove Duluth Road and then McMaster, and finally Bruce so she could hole up inside her tiny slate-colored apartment, one tear dribbled out the corner of her eye. She scrubbed it gone and her face was clean. *God handles messiness*, she thought.

After parking, she listened to Beyoncé sing about freedom, and then she grabbed her purse.

The walk was lined with zinnias and she was feeling better. The air was a relief, or maybe that was just her soul settling. A bird caught her attention, a sparrow, and she followed it in the sky then glanced at her porch to see if her monthly hair care products had been delivered. Instead, she saw Macon's lazy shape and she instantly brightened. It wasn't the worst day after all. Randi was with him, and when Lucy approached the two of them, her daughter waved her arms as if this moment was the best in her life and she was happy to see Lucy still standing.

# Bios

**Herina Ayot** is Kenyan American, a mother of twins, a lover of everything beautiful, and a storyteller documenting her journey through life. She writes about the difficult places. Her personal essays and nonfiction have appeared in Ebony Magazine, The Root, Human Parts, and The Huffington Post. Herina was a 2014 Hurston/Wright Fellow and the 2019 winner of NYU's Threesis Academic Challenge where she discussed her novel in progress that centers on themes of victim and perpetrator, childhood trauma, and redemption. She holds a BA in Psychology with a minor in Journalism and an MFA in Creative Writing from NYU. She lives in the New York Metropolitan area with her sons and her girl pup, Nikki Giovanni. Find her work at herinaayot.com and follow her on Instagram @herinaayot.

**angelia carey** is a reader, writer, and chef (not always in that order), and she cares if you ate today. an adult beginner who's proud not to have a calling. descendant of cow people. not horse people.

**Abigail Jordon** attended the University of Southern Mississippi where she studied English Licensure and graduated in May 2022. Her passion for writing began at a young age. Her family is from Guyana, South America, making her a first-generation American. She grew up writing and illustrating every story that came to mind. Her grandfather was a writer; she believes she gets it from him. Her family is incredible and has always supported her writing endeavors. She hopes to work in the publishing industry as a young, Black female, to help diversify the field. She would love to work with children's books, advocating for representation and diversity. Ultimately, she wants to be a writer and tell stories that haven't been told yet to little boys and girls that look like her.

**Quintessa Knight** is an Atlanta-based writer with works published in *Hayden's Ferry Review* and *Dear America: Reflections on Race*. Through an introverted and awkward disposition, she finds her connection with readers through the nostalgia of growing up Black with stories that highlight Black protagonists in the otherness they feel trapped in from their communities and/or society. She is currently working on her first novel of superpowered POC. When she's not working, she is reading other Black authors that inspire her, learning to be a better plant mom, and falling into the depths of geek culture. She can be found on Instagram @quintessaknight.

**Valerie Morales** has reviewed books for the digital platform Book Browse, specializing in BIPOC stories, for the past three years. Other work has been showcased on digital platforms such as Huffington Post, The Talented Tenth Review on Medium, The Committed Generation, and in the periodical The Women's Review of Books.

**Chinwe I. Ndubuka's** flash fiction and short stories have appeared in *Interpretations*, the anthology of the Columbia Art League; *Well Versed*, the anthology of the Columbia Chapter of the Missouri Writers' Guild (CCMWG); and *Evening Street Review*. "Week Two and Counting" won a themed flash fiction contest organized by the Daniel Boone Regional Library. Chinwe is a member of the CCMWG.

**Hannah Onoguwe's** work has appeared in The Missing Slate, The Stockholm Review, Omenana, Timeworn Lit Mag, Eleven Eleven, and the Strange Lands Short Stories from Flame Tree Publishing among others. She was shortlisted for the 2020 Afritondo Short Story Prize and has work forthcoming on Mysterion. She lives in Yenagoa with her family where she often finds time to bake. You can find her on Twitter, Facebook and Instagram @HannahOnoguwe.

**Ifediba Zube** writes from Abuja Nigeria. She has been published in the Forge Literary Magazine and elsewhere.

# About The Editor

Ianna A. Small is the founder of midnight & indigo Publishing and creator of *midnight & indigo*, a literary platform dedicated to short stories and narrative essays by Black women writers. m&i is her love letter to Black women like herself, who long to reach the pinnacle of their purpose. As the executive editor of midnight & indigo, she oversees editorial and creative direction for the digital and print platforms, and recruitment for the *midnight & indigo* Writing Studio, which offers craft and genre-based online classes for Black writers. A media marketing executive, Ms. Small has 20+ years of experience developing marketing strategies, partnerships, distribution and content marketing initiatives for major entertainment brands including BET, Disney Channel, ESPN, ABC, FX, Nat Geo, VH1, MTV, HOT97, and others.

An avid fan of Black and South Asian literature, Korean horror, and all things Jesus + Michelle Obama + The Golden Girls + cultural food documentaries, she dreams of one day running midnight & indigo from a lounge chair overlooking the archipelagos of Santorini, her happy place.

Ms. Small is a proud graduate of Syracuse University and active member of ACES: The Society for Editing and the EFA (Editorial Freelancers Organization). She is a granddaughter to Irma, daughter to Nadia, and mother to Jalen Anthony, who is simply: her reason.

Made in the USA
Middletown, DE
17 May 2022